LEGACY

David Berardelli

LEGACY

GRAVESTONE PRESS

DAY ONE

Chapter 1

Julie spent the entire flight home thinking about her latest trip to Moundsville, where she'd gone to pay her respects to her grandmother by visiting the lovely lady's grave.

It had been a bright, sunny morning. It was late in the summer, and the nights had been getting cooler. She was grateful that she'd had the foresight to bring her lightweight jacket to the cemetery, which sat in quiet solitude in the middle of an open field. The wind whispering somberly from the pine forest directly west of the place had caused a moderately chilly afternoon in the Ohio Valley.

She thought it very strange that she could face the lady's grave and not feel completely devastated by the loss of her friend. The sadness was quite substantial, of course, and would always be, as was the tremendous sense of loss, which had caused a heavy throbbing in the pit of her stomach. Yet the feeling that her grandmother's spirit remained by her side seemed very real. When Julie placed her palm on the cold stone marker, she strongly felt that her grandmother's hand had come down from wherever her spirit now rested, filling her being with a tender warmth she would never be able to describe.

Julie closed her eyes and smiled as the warmth flowed gently through her.

I miss you, my dear friend...but I will always feel your closeness...

Although the sweet old woman was gone, many signs of her remained, and could be experienced in the sprawling West Virginia hillside. Birds chirped, flitting from tree to tree. Traffic sounds, most likely caused by the heavily traveled I-70, had been hushed considerably by the breeze blowing through the woods.

Gram had lived in the boonies all her life and had never been fond of traffic sounds. Julie had always thought it very strange that even though her grandmother lived just a few miles from the Interstate, the woods surrounding the small farm never failed to keep the irritating sounds of civilization from invading her quiet sanctuary.

Julie smiled lovingly at the bouquet of roses she'd placed on the grass in front of the smooth gray marker, knowing she'd be back the next year with a fresh batch. She'd been visiting the sweet lady each year since her old college days and saw no reason to stop the tradition. Just because the woman was no longer among the living shouldn't mean Julie needed to end the visits, did it?

"Rest in peace, sweet lady." Julie shivered at the sudden catch in her throat. "I'll always love you, and I'll be back again next year." She blew a kiss at the marker, then turned to walk down the winding dirt path that would take her back to the rental car.

Just as she was about to reach out for the driver's door, a magnificent monarch butterfly flitted over and landed on the tip of the antenna. It

6

stood there, watching her, perched at a slight angle, its beautiful wings rising and falling slowly.

Gram loved butterflies.

"You've probably already seen her," she whispered, smiling. "I'll bet she's already given you a name."

It cocked its tiny round head as if it were actually listening. Then, just moments later, it left its perch and flitted back up the hill. It paused for a moment as it reached her grandmother's marker, then swooped up in a wide arc and disappeared among the trees.

I really should've known, Julie thought. *She was bound to make friends with everyone long before now.*

Her eyes moist, Julie slid behind the wheel of the rental and drove back to her motel that awaited her just a few miles from downtown Wheeling.

***

Robert didn't notice the slender brunette until he nearly slammed her to the ground while rushing blindly out of the terminal to hunt down a cab.

He'd just gotten off the plane a few minutes before. He'd had no problem picking up his single piece of luggage at Baggage Claim. In no time he'd joined the scattered, slow-moving crowds that had been creating an obstacle course throughout the terminal. His head was filled with muddled images of the software convention he'd attended in Miami as he hustled toward the EXIT signs and turned right, where the large sliding glass doors awaited him just ten yards away.

As he scurried to the entrance, his attention focused on getting out his cell to let his secretary Mildred know he was on his way back to the office. He was surprised she hadn't already called him. She knew which flight he'd taken and would certainly want to know when he'd be back to conduct business.

He was fumbling for his phone when he turned right, where the open entrance led to the thruway out front, showing a long line of taxis waiting for fares.

At that same moment, more than half a dozen others dashed outside, among them, a tall, slender brunette in a black skirt, a blue long-sleeve blouse, and open-toed black pumps. She was carrying a large tan handbag and pulling a smallish gray suitcase on wheels behind her.

As she drew closer, Richard bumped into her left shoulder, nearly knocking her down. Despite her pumps, which forced her ankles to bend sharply, she managed to stay on her feet. However, her awkward position had twisted her shoulder, causing her to lose her grip on the suitcase. It flipped over and slid toward the curb. The strap of her handbag dropped down her left arm and broke loose, sending the bag to the ground at his feet.

Robert's jaw dropped when he realized what had happened.

"Damn! I'm so *sorry*!" His pulse hammered as he hurriedly shoved the cell back into his pocket. He dropped his own suitcase, then quickly bent to grab hers. He brought it over, then picked up her handbag. Her checkbook and two ballpoint pens had escaped the confines of the bag and lay on the concrete, near the curb. He snatched those up as well. Then he spun around and scurried back over, nearly slamming her in the cheek when he held out her bag.

She managed to jerk out of the way just as the large, heavy object sailed past, missing her jaw by inches.

Feeling like a blundering idiot, Robert stood perfectly still, holding her checkbook and pens in one hand and her bag in the other while swarms of people rushed past, in search of a cab.

"You okay?" She sounded concerned.

He couldn't believe what she'd just asked. He'd nearly put her in the hospital, for God's sake. But now she was asking him if *he* was okay. Very strange. It made him feel slightly less of an idiot, knowing that this beautiful young woman didn't want to strangle him for nearly slamming her to the ground, then attempting to knock her unconscious with her own bag. He was just grateful that she hadn't flown into a violent tirade of insults and physical rage.

Even so, he couldn't believe what he had just done. This sort of thing had never happened to him before. But as humiliating as it was, he somehow didn't feel nearly as badly as he thought he should. It no doubt had something to do with her large, beautiful blue eyes, which were totally fixed on him. Besides their obvious hypnotic quality, their gentle gaze reassured him that she wasn't enraged by his clumsiness, as most others certainly would be.

9

"Well? *Are* you all right? You look a little, well, bummed out."

"I *think* I'm okay. At least, I *hope* I am."

"You look all right…mostly. A little flushed, maybe. Embarrassed?"

"Does it show much?"

She smiled. "Only on your face and the way you keep standing there, not moving."

He smiled awkwardly. "I'm afraid to."

"Really?"

"I don't want to start moving around and accidentally poke out one of your eyes."

"Don't be so hard on yourself. Stuff like this happens to everyone."

"This has happened to you, too?"

"No, but I thought I should at least try making you feel less of a schmuck."

"Gee, thanks…"

She chuckled and gave him a wink.

He couldn't stop gazing at those beautiful eyes. They were the largest, the clearest, the brightest shade of blue he had ever seen. He quickly discovered that he could not turn away from them. It took him even less time to realize that he didn't *want* to.

This girl was quite striking. She appeared to be about twenty-five, maybe twenty-eight. She had a dazzling smile, and her laugh was infectious.

But those eyes…

He just couldn't get over them. They were so clear, so bright… They pulled you right in, making you wonder if she possessed supernatural powers.

They stared at one another for what seemed—at least to him—a very long time. Then she shrugged. "May I please have my things?" She pointed to her bag. "I kinda need them for, you know, important stuff? Identification? Taking out a credit card to buy something pretty? Or maybe a cheeseburger? That sorta thing? And yes, I have been known to write a check every now and then. You've got that covered, too."

He looked down. He was still holding her bag, checkbook, and pens.

This made him feel even more like an idiot.

He groaned. "Again, I'm really and truly—"

"It's all right." She took her bag, dropped the pens and checkbook inside, snapped the bag shut, and slid the strap onto her left shoulder. "And don't beat yourself up, okay? It was just an accident." She tilted her head, which forced some dark brown hair to slide down her front. "You didn't do it intentionally, did you?"

He shook his head and suddenly realized that he could spend the rest of the day staring at those eyes.

"You have a nice day, all right? And *please* watch where you're going from now on? I'd hate for you to slam into someone else, someone who isn't as nice—or as forgiving—as I am." She laughed.

"I'll try. You have a nice day, too." He watched as she turned and headed on over to an awaiting cab, her hair bouncing on her shoulders.

Just then, he remembered that he needed a ride, too. He scoured the line of cabs. Every one of them began pulling away from the curb.

The brunette opened the door of the cab, paused, then turned back around. "I'm sorry. You were here first, weren't you? That is, you would've been, if you hadn't, you know..." She shrugged a shoulder and smiled. "Nearly flattened me."

He couldn't help laughing. "It's all right. I owe you."

"For what?"

"For, you know..."

"Nearly crippling me? Blinding me? Knocking me unconscious?"

He nodded. "That's an excellent way of explaining our little tryst..."

"But you didn't. Not really. I'm still right here, breathing just fine, standing up, moving around—all on my own."

"Give me another chance. I'm sure I can mess you up in ways you could never imagine in a million years." He had no idea why he'd said that. But it was well worth it. She laughed again, this time even harder.

He found himself lost once again in those eyes. This girl was not only stunning, but she was also a delight to be with. Had he seen a wedding ring? A band, perhaps? He hadn't noticed. Her eyes had blown him away, and he seemed to ignore most everything else. But right now, he didn't seem to care. He was much too busy fantasizing about getting in the cab with her.

12

"C'mon, I don't bite." She gestured to the open door.

"Aren't you afraid *I* do?"

"It's all right. I've had my shots."

He hurried over. The cabby came around, took their suitcases, and placed them carefully in the trunk. Robert slid in after her and pulled the door shut.

The taxi eased away from the curb.

Chapter 2

"I'm Julie. Julie Kenner." She held out her hand. It was slender and warm, her grip firm.

"Robert Townsend."

"What do your friends call you? Robert? Bob?"

"What makes you think I have any friends?"

"Just hoping you do, Robert. Or Bob."

"If I *had* any friends, I'd want them to call me Bob. But since I don't spend much time socializing, I really don't have many at all. Mostly everyone calls me Robert." He wondered why she hoped he had friends. "Why would you care, by the way?"

Her dark brows came together. "I'd hate to share a cab with someone who has no friends."

"Well, I do have one or two, so it's okay to stay in the cab with me. What do yours call you?"

"My *good* friends call me Julie. My *uppity* ones call me Jewels."

"You have uppity friends?"

"No, but I'm hopeful."

"Hopeful?"

"I've always wanted to tell someone not to call me Jewels."

"An uppity wouldn't take too kindly to that."

"Then I could tell them to leave me alone."

"I've always liked women who call their own shots."

"Where you two headed?" the cabby asked in a high-pitched, raspy voice.

"Winter Park," Julie said. "I'll let you know where you can drop me off on Park Avenue. I run a

14

flower shop there and better make an appearance—just to make sure my assistant hasn't closed up early, as she usually does when I'm not right there, watching her struggle to develop a work ethic."

"And you?" The cabby was eyeing him in the mirror.

"Maguire Boulevard. My complex is right across the street from Fashion Square." He turned to Julie. "How long have you had your shop?"

"About two years, now. You work in one of those business centers on Maguire?"

"I own and run T&S Software Associates. We're brokers, and I usually have to attend a convention once or twice a month to make sure I'm up to speed with the latest innovations. That's one of the many irritating things about technology. There are always innovations."

"They have a bunch of those conventions in Miami, don't they?"

"Usually. I've had to attend them a few times in Tampa and St. Pete, and I had to fly to L.A. a couple of times, but mostly Miami."

"You like Miami?"

"I like it a lot better than L.A."

She smiled. "Because it's a much shorter flight?"

"I take it you can tell that I hate flying."

She nodded.

"It's that obvious?"

"You kinda bared your teeth when you mentioned L.A."

"I don't like flying, but I really hate L.A."

She nodded. "I understand."

"Do you really?"

"Sure do. The bared teeth thing unnerved me a little."

"Now I feel like a wolf."

"Well, you *are* a *guy*… And you *did* almost flatten me back there…"

"Ouch. Anyway, that's not fair." He knew she was kidding the instant she broke out in laughter. He shook his head. "You really had me going there. For a second."

"That long?"

"Sometimes I'm not exactly what you'd call quick."

"I guess this is one of those sometimes, then?"

"Definitely."

"What makes this occasion different?"

"Beautiful women do things to me."

"Thank you. You mean mental things? Or is this an issue we can't discuss in a cab?"

"Uh-huh…"

She laughed. "You know, this conversation seems to be making you out to be silly."

"I don't mean to be…"

She looked confused. "This is *natural* for you?"

"Only because you're tormenting me about trying to kill you back there."

"You think I'm tormenting you?"

"Aren't you?"

"I thought I was just teasing."

"You always tease strange guys in taxis?"

"You're not *that* strange…"

He laughed.

"You've never been told that before?"

16

"Only by my mother. And several ex-girlfriends, as well as a therapist or two."

"No ex-wives talk badly about you?"

"It's hard to talk badly when you don't even exist."

She gazed at him for a moment. "How about a present one?"

"You mean wife?"

"That would be a good example..."

"As in right now? This minute?"

"We've been riding around in this cab for more than a minute, you know. Let's try for the last six months or so and see where it gets us."

"No wife. Or ex-wife. Not even an almost-a-wife."

"A nice-looking guy like you?"

"Hard to believe any decent babe in her right mind could turn down *this* poster boy for virility, ain't it?"

"You're really full of yourself, but you're right." She sounded serious.

He began to wonder if he had just accidentally slipped into Everyman's special dream.

"What do you do that turns them off?"

"Whaddya mean?"

"I mean, are you into anything weird? Kinky stuff? Or do you do disgusting things when you're eating, or making love?"

"I can be kinky on occasion."

"What occasion?"

"Whenever the lady wishes."

She nodded. "Sounds reasonable. What else?"

"You wanna know about the eating thing?"

"If there *is* one…"

"I like separating my carrots from the peas."

"Why?"

"It just looks better. More orderly."

"Ah. You're OCD."

"Not really."

"But you just said—"

"I'm kidding."

She shook her head.

"Really. I honestly don't like carrots."

"They're good for you."

"I know. That eyesight thingy, right?"

Long before they realized it, the cab slowed down.

"Which one?" the cabby asked as he pulled into the turnoff lane on Maguire.

"Damn. We're here already?" Robert's heart sank. This trip ended much too quickly.

"Where do we go?"

Robert sighed deeply and took one last long look at those gorgeous blue eyes. He wanted the cabby to head straight to Park Avenue, drop Julie off, then come back.

Would that be too bold? Or should he arrange to meet with her later on?

A glance at his watch told him he should already be back at the office.

Somehow, he didn't care about the office right now. He took in her lavender scent and knew he'd hate himself forever if he didn't change the itinerary. "Let's drop you off first, okay?"

She blinked. "But we're already here…"

"He can turn around and bring me back." Robert glanced at the cabby. "Can't you?"

The man shrugged. "Don't mind payin' extra?"

"I don't mind at all."

"We be in business, then…" The cabby pulled back onto Maguire.

Julie was watching him. "Won't this make you late, getting back to your office?"

"It sure will."

She laughed. "If I didn't know better, I'd think that you really didn't *want* to get back."

"And you'd be absolutely right."

"Seriously?"

"Let's see…" He pushed his brows together. "Getting back to the office and arguing with arrogant people for the next three hours? Or spending fifteen more minutes with a gorgeous woman?" He shrugged. "How do ya think that one should play out?"

She shook her head. "I feel sorry for your employees."

"Feel sorry for *me*. *I'm* the one they're always dumping on."

"Been there, believe me." She opened her bag and reached inside. "Wanna hook up some time?"

He had no idea how to respond.. This beautiful creature was asking him out. On a date.

She pulled out a thick beige wallet. "You're not saying anything."

He kept staring. "You're right. I hear that same batch of crickets."

Her eyes grew. "Does that mean yes? No? Maybe? You don't know? You *do* know, but you're

19

not sure? I'm not your type?" A shrug. "Give me a clue, okay? Toss me something before I start feeling insecure. I get kinda cranky when I feel insecure."

"We wouldn't want *that*, would we?"

"Heavens, no. Especially since we've just met. I do have standards, you know…"

"All righty, then. Let's get back to answering your questions. Yes, I want to hook up. Yes, you are most definitely my type. And here's one extra, while we're on the subject. You're not married?"

"If I was, I wouldn't want to hook up with a strange man, would I?"

"That depends."

She shrugged. "On what?"

"On how strange *you* are."

"And if I'm not?"

"What? Strange? Or married?"

"I *almost* was… Married, that is."

"Then that means no, right?"

"That would mean no, yes."

"Good answer."

"So then, you wanna hook up sometime later?"

"No, but sometime very, very *soon* would be just great."

She handed him a card. It had her name on it, the name of the flower shop, and her shop phone number. There was also a modernized stencil image of a bouquet of roses positioned in the center of the card, beneath the name of the shop. "My home phone number's written on the back."

"You hand these out to every guy you meet in a cab?" He pulled out his wallet and very carefully slipped the card inside.

"Yes."

He flinched. "Really?"

"You're the only guy I've ever met in one."

"I guess that makes me special, then…"

"I'm pretty sure you really are, actually." She held out her hand.

He looked at it.

"What's wrong now?"

"I'm wondering what you want me to do."

"You really are silly—did you know that?"

"You've already said that."

"I mean it."

"Okay, but what does that have to do with your hand?"

"Don't *you* have a card?"

He groaned. "I really *am* an idiot."

"Yes, but does this mean you *do* have a card? And that you're about to give it to me sometime soon?"

"Like now, you mean?"

"Now would be just fine. Later might not be too convenient—especially if I'm no longer sitting here with you."

He opened his wallet, pulled out a card, and handed it over.

She looked at it. "Impressive. It makes you sound, well, less like an idiot."

"Thanks a lot."

She held out her hand again. This time, he knew what to do. He took it and held it for several moments, thinking, *Where have you been all my life, Julie Kenner*?

"Waiting for someone like you to come along," she replied softly.

He recoiled. "How did you *do* that?"

"Do what?"

"You…just read my mind!"

A slight smile. "I don't do minds, I do expressions."

"My *expression* told you all that?"

"It was enough, believe me."

"Whatever you're doing obviously works."

She just shrugged.

He sat in silence, enjoying the feel of her hand.

A few moments later, she tilted her head and smiled. "May I have it back? Please? I promise I'll take good care of it."

Reluctantly he let her go and continued focusing on her eyes.

"What are you doing Friday night?" he asked, his heart pounding.

"Spending it with you?"

"Great answer."

"Actually, there was a question mark tagging along at the end of it."

"Okay, then. The answer to that would be a definite yes, I can't wait, and Friday can't come fast enough. How's *that* for spontaneity?"

"We're comin' up to Park Avenue," the cabby said as they proceeded through the busy intersection. "You wanna tell me the address?"

Julie's eyes suddenly filled the sockets.

Robert noticed that she'd stiffened in her seat. "Julie? What's wrong?"

"Stop the car!" The volume of her voice made the interior of the cab vibrate.

Robert pulled back.

The cabby jumped and half turned. "Wha—?"

"Just *stop*!"

Robert shivered as his blood turned cold.

Julie yelled, "*Now*!" at the top of her lungs.

The cabby mashed down on the brake pedal.

A deafening roar. An ear-splitting screeching of brakes.

Straight ahead, a red blur whizzed by and immediately smashed brutally into the driver's side of the oncoming light gray SUV, welding it and a red Camaro into a single grotesque entity sliding sideways at lightning speed.

Chapter 3

The intersection looked like a bomb had gone off.

Jagged pieces of plastic and shards of shattered glass glittered like precious gems in the street and at the curb. The front of the red Camaro had been crushed accordion-style. The glass from the windshield, shattered by the impact, had been slammed into the interior, covering the driver.

The driver's side of the SUV was smashed into oblivion, forcing the vehicle into a grotesquely uneven L shape. Broken glass and pieces of silver and chrome winked in the afternoon sunlight. The streetlamp struck by the collision was bent into a 45% angle. Its glass domes had exploded, raining down on the awning of a woman's dress shop before scattering onto the sidewalk and in the street.

At least two people remained in the wreckage but showed no signs of life.

Julie sat back in her seat and forced her nerves to settle down.

She hoped she hadn't messed up things with Robert. She'd known a lot of guys in her twenty-eight years and had learned that, with certain things, they tended to react the same way. In this case, men often freaked out whenever they suspected the girl they were with turned out to be anything but ordinary.

Even though Julie considered her special gift extraordinary to most, she sincerely hoped this solitary incident wouldn't end what could easily blossom into something special.

What was it she possessed, anyway? A highly developed sixth sense? An acutely formed intuition? An incredible sense of impending doom?

Certainly nothing worth freaking out about—especially since she had just saved two other lives.

Countless others, as she'd learned through personal research over the years, also possessed a sixth sense. Still others were gifted with even more outlandish abilities, such as musical genius, brilliance in math, speed-reading abilities, and more bizarre skills, such as communicating with the dead. Compared with such superior skills, Julie's unique little gift could hardly be considered for mention in the Guinness Book of World Records.

It was a shame she couldn't have helped the unfortunates in the Camaro and the SUV. But doing something like that would have been just short of miraculous. How on earth could she possibly stop others from killing or hurting each other?

It was enough that the three of them had managed to avoid death. So why was she feeling so self-conscious about this?

Was it because of Robert? Was she worried that she had just met someone very special and in doing her thing, had jinxed the natural course of events? Or did she think Robert, like all the other young men she had dealt with in the past, might freak at this as well?

Right now, he was gazing at the mess across the street. She could tell by the rigid way he was sitting that he was struggling to comprehend what had just happened.

She tapped him gently on the shoulder.

He jumped.

"You okay?" she asked.

He shook his head and blinked. She sensed by the blankness in his eyes that he didn't recognize her. But when she smiled at him, the blankness vanished, and he sighed. However, she could tell that he was confused and somewhat shocked by the strange situation.

He shook himself. "I...think so..."

A crowd had appeared, flocking around the wreckage. Cell phones sparkled in the sun, clicking madly, like hordes of fireflies.

The cabby was rubbing his eyes.

"Are *you* all right?" Julie asked him.

"H-How'd ya know?" Squinting, he turned to her. She sensed his confusion.

"Pardon?"

"H-How'd ya know we had to stop?"

She shrugged. "Just a feeling I had."

"You saved our lives, ya know..."

Julie turned back to the wreckage. "I couldn't save *them*..."

Two policemen got out of a squad car and hurried over to the debris. They were trying to open the driver's door of the Camaro when the EM unit arrived.

"I'm just damn glad we stopped." The cabby shook his head. "If I'd argued with ya a second longer—"

"You didn't, so don't even go there."

The cabby was about to say something else when another cop crossed the street, heading in their direction.

Robert was staring at Julie again.

She sensed what was coming. Something wasn't making sense to him. He wanted to ask about it but seemed hesitant.

Just as she was about to reassure him, the cop tapped on the cabby's window.

***

"You say the Camaro missed you by maybe a foot?"

The cop was about forty, stood about six-three, and weighed at least two hundred pounds. His nametag said *BELSON*. He was writing busily into his notepad but stopped frequently, as if he had forgotten something.

The cabby said, "I could feel its breeze shake the hell out of us when she flew by!"

The cop continued scribbling. "And ya say your light was green when the Camaro ran the intersection?"

"Yeah."

"You were proceeding on green, then." The cop turned to Robert.

Robert couldn't stand still. His nerves were still shaky. It was difficult for him to pull his gaze away from the mess just a hundred yards or so to his left. "I believe so," he said uneasily.

The cop stopped writing. He stared at Robert. "You *believe* so?"

Robert sighed. He knew he should start making sense. Cops always seemed to be suspicious—

27

especially if something didn't exactly sound right. "Officer, at this point, I have no idea *what* the hell happened. I didn't even hear the damned thing coming at us. If it hadn't been for Ms. Kenner, here—"

"I just saw it out of the corner of my eye." Julie shrugged. "I guess my timing turned out to be really great."

Robert sincerely hoped she was telling the truth. He sensed she was holding something back. Something he needed to know. It was obviously important, since whatever it was had just saved three lives.

"Great peripheral vision, maybe?" The cop raised his dark brows.

She smiled sheepishly.

Robert was suspicious of her attitude. Her expression somehow suggested that she had not been joking and might indeed be hiding something. In his view, the Mustang had been moving entirely too fast for the cabby to see it and bring the cab to an abrupt stop at the last second. Yet Julie had somehow seen it and reacted much more quickly.

And had obviously done it in plenty of time to save their lives.

"The light was green, then, Miss?"

"Definitely."

"And the other car—the SUV—was coming from the north? And was also moving on green?"

"Yes. The Camaro zipped through the light on red. It didn't even slow down."

"Any idea how you managed to stop in time?" The cop had stopped writing and began watching the cabby.

"*She* told me to stop." He jabbed a thumb at Julie.

The cop looked skeptical.

"Actually, she *screamed* for me to stop."

The cop was clearly confused. "But if the Camaro was moving that fast—"

"If she hadn't screamed at me," the cabby said, "I could *never* have stopped in time."

"But you obviously did."

"We didn't get hit, did we?"

"Miss?" The cop shrugged. "Does this sound accurate?"

"It's what saved us."

Robert went over the nightmare in his head once again. He really wanted to believe that the cabby had indeed mashed down on the brakes at the last moment to avoid the crash because Julie had screamed for him to do it…

But even though he was confident that he remembered what had happened, he discovered that this major detail had scurried off into the dark nothingness that had taken over his thoughts ever since that moment, when he had nearly smashed his face into the front seat headrest.

"This explains how your cab cleared the path," the cop said. "But if the Camaro was moving that fast, it was sheer luck that you were able to stop in time."

The cabby nodded.

Robert wasn't so sure. He knew he should just be satisfied that the three of them were still alive. *How* it happened really shouldn't matter *that* much, should it?

"Anything to add?" The cop was watching him closely.

"Do we need to follow you back to the Station?" Robert wanted to get this over with. Standing here like this was making him uncomfortable.

"No, sir. I think we've got all we need. Two eyewitnesses have corroborated your story, and they both said you had the green. The liability clearly lies with the Camaro, but it doesn't look like she's gonna be much help."

"Then we can go?"

The cop nodded. "I've got your info. We might be calling you in the next few days if we need ya." He snapped his notepad shut. "Thanks for your cooperation." He turned and hurried over to the other two cops, who were still managing crowd activity.

"You guys okay?" Julie asked.

"Thanks to you I am, lady!" The cabby grinned at her.

Robert was watching the paramedics as they slid the gurney into the rear of their mobile medical unit. "I'm not sure."

"No?"

He took a breath. "Not really."

"I'm really sorry this happened."

"It wasn't exactly your fault, you know."

"I know, but it still shook you up."

Something suddenly occurred to him, and he wanted to yell at himself for being so selfish. Julie had gone through this nightmare, too. But for some stupid reason, he was acting almost like she was the one who'd caused it. He needed to stop being a moron and start acting like his old self again. "How about you?"

"I'm fine."

"You're sure?"

"I'm positive. Why? Don't I look okay?"

"You look much better than okay."

She smiled. "I take it we're still on for Friday, then?"

Her question surprised him. "What would make you think otherwise?"

She shrugged. "That bummed-out expression on your face…"

"How's this?" He gave her a dazzling smile.

She shook her head. "About three or four notches over the top."

"How about this?" He toned it down a tad with a mildly pleasant half-smile. And a wink.

"*Much* better."

"The wink a tad much?"

She tilted her head and looked thoughtful.

"Too much, huh?"

"At this stage? I'll gladly take it."

Chapter 4

Robert entered the T&S offices at a few minutes past two, just as Mildred put down the phone.

She made a quick note on her pad and looked up at him over her reading glasses. As he expected, she made her usual deadpan observation, her cultured red brows mashing together as she quickly evaluated him. "How'd the convention go?"

"Nothing special. Miss me?"

"Terribly." It was said dryly.

"I can tell. You look sort of miserable. You knew I'd be back, right?"

She said nothing.

"Let me guess. *That's* why you're so miserable, right?"

She ignored that one—which told him she had a lot of things on her mind. "You're running late. I expected you back before lunch. Was it traffic again? Your flight was on time. I checked."

His first reaction was to tell her that he couldn't call her because he was much too busy trying to figure out why he and two other people hadn't been smeared all over Semoran Avenue.

He decided not to tell her about the accident. Or about Julie. He didn't want to tell her anything that he couldn't fully understand himself. And even though he hadn't thought much about anything else since, he still wasn't sure if he was more confused about what should have happened but didn't, or how

32

Julie had actually seen the Camaro in plenty of time, as she had told them.

Forget it. You're alive. She's alive. The cab driver's alive. Does it matter that what Julie had done didn't in any way seem humanly possible? The fact that it happened in the very best possible way should be enough, shouldn't it?

He kept telling himself that his reasoning was right. Everything turned out okay, so what was the problem?

Was it the way it happened that bothered him?

Or was it the time element that just didn't make any sense?

"Robert?" Mildred's crinkly brow suggested that she was growing impatient. "Everything all right?"

"Colonial traffic was kind of hectic. Any calls?"

"There were two for you specifically. The first one was from that guy from Prudential who wants you to buy more insurance. I believe this was his third or fourth call over the last two weeks."

"Did you tell him I'm not interested?"

"I already told him three times. I saw no reason to try for a fourth. I decided to let you do it when he calls back."

"Think he'll call back?"

"He said he would. Since he's already tried so many times before, I think he'll be good to his word…"

"Lucky me. Who else called?"

"Ms. Watts wanted to talk to you."

Carolyn. Terrific. This isn't what I need right now.

He'd just started dating her a couple of weeks ago. Carolyn was a nice girl, but since he'd just met Julie, he hadn't thought of Carolyn and saw no reason to lead her on. Even though he had spent what amounted to less than an hour with Julie, his gut—as well as his heart—told him she could quite possibly be The One. And if this were true, he didn't want Carolyn wasting her time with someone who was no longer interested.

"Did she say what she wanted?" He knew better than to ask but decided to, anyway. Just in case Carolyn had something else on her mind.

"No. And I didn't ask."

"That was nice of you."

"I thought so, too. You know how I am about minding my own business."

"Vividly." He'd mentioned having dinner with Carolyn when he got back from Miami. But now that Julie was in the picture, he knew this wouldn't work. It would be cruel to take Carolyn anywhere while his mind was fixed on someone else. Most guys wouldn't think twice about doing such a thing. He wasn't one of them.

Even so, he hated himself. He had had two great dates with Carolyn, and he liked her. And to make matters even more complicated, he knew she liked him as well.

But that didn't seem to matter right now.

His office smelled strongly of freshly brewed coffee. Once again he was grateful that Mildred loved coffee as much as he did and always kept a pot brewed for him. He poured a cup.

On the other side of the heavily tinted window, Central Florida winked blinding stars of sunlight from the windows of the neighboring buildings and the windshields of the vehicles cluttering up the parking lots and the straight stretch of Maguire Boulevard.

He circled his desk, sat, and picked up his cell. Just as he was about to press Carolyn's number, his thoughts immediately focused on thick dark brown hair and large, clear blue eyes. And, of course, that dazzling smile.

The moment Julie's picture had drifted into his thoughts, he put down the cell and picked up his mug. For the next fifteen minutes, he thought of her smile, their wonderful exchange in the cab, her wit, her expression the moment he nearly smacked her in the face with her handbag...

And those eyes.

Those big, beautiful, shimmering blue eyes that centered on you and penetrated your most intimate thoughts...

The image came back to him in a flash. Before he realized it, he was wondering once again where he could take her for dinner.

Then, in the middle of his daydreaming, his cell buzzed.

The display quickly gave him the bad news: *C. Watts*.

His pulse raced as he slowly placed the phone to his ear. He sighed tiredly and forced himself to focus on what he had to say to the lady. "Hi."

"Forget about me? Or are you just busy?"

"I just got back from the airport."

"Mildred told me when you were getting back. Everything okay?"

"Everything's just fine."

"Are we still on for tonight?"

Damn. He'd hoped it had somehow slipped her mind. But he knew better. Women just didn't forget such things.

"Tonight?" he asked uneasily.

"Tonight. Uh-huh. You know. It's actually today, but if you add three or four hours to it to allow for the rest of the workday, then another hour or so to drive home and change clothes, it automatically becomes tonight."

He didn't reply.

"You're not saying anything."

The very same words Julie had said not more than an hour ago.

Once again, he found his mind focusing on their encounter, but before he could settle on something—

"I'm not getting a warm fuzzy about this," she said flatly.

He felt even more like a cold-hearted bastard. Carolyn was a sweet, intelligent, classy lady. She worked her butt off at her insurance office on Robinson as well as in the gym and had a fantastic butt as the result of her efforts.

He began thinking about Julie's butt and found himself once again focusing on her beautiful eyes.

"You're still not saying anything." Carolyn sighed tiredly. "This is telling me a little too much

36

about that warm fuzzy I've been anxiously waiting for."

His thoughts looped. He didn't want to hurt Carolyn's feelings but knew there was no way he could handle this that would turn the exchange into anything pleasant or amiable. Carolyn had obviously been looking forward to the evening and deserved a special night out. But he couldn't think of that right now. He had no choice but tell her the truth. He owed her that much.

"Carolyn, I've got to tell you something…"

"Uh-oh…"

"I really need to—"

"Lemme save you the trouble. You've met someone."

He nearly gasped. "H-How'd you know?"

"Let's just say it was pretty obvious."

"Obvious?"

"When you remind a guy about a date and he doesn't say anything, it's a red flag just by itself. But when he suddenly breaks the silence by telling you something that you're pretty sure has got nothing to do with the details of the date? Well, I'll let you figure that one out all by yourself…"

"I'm really sorry."

"I know."

"I hope you can understand."

"Oh, I understand, all right."

"You do?"

"Of course. It's called life, and everyone knows life can be great sometimes and really suck other times. But I do understand. I don't like it very much at all. In fact, I hate it…but yes, I understand."

"I didn't plan on this, by the way."

"Robert, both you and I know that most terrible things that happen in life aren't exactly planned."

"Terrible?"

"In this case? For me. But not for you, obviously."

He just sighed and continued to feel like a bastard.

"Nothing else to say, is there?"

"Just that I'm really—"

"I know. You're sorry."

"I really am."

"So am I. See ya in the next life, then?"

"Or maybe in this one?"

"Maybe…*if* I'm still not mad at you. And *if* you're free again. And if *I'm* free as well. And, of course, *if* I've forgiven you."

"It's a date, then?"

"Not funny, Robert."

"Just trying to—"

"Lighten the moment?"

He felt terribly bad and guilty and hated himself. He imagined she hated him even more. "Uh, something like that."

"Don't bother. I get it. Have a great life, Robert."

***

Robert spent the rest of the afternoon on the phone, handling conference calls.

It turned out to be a welcomed relief, enabling him to get his mind off his recent breakup with Carolyn. When he stopped thinking of her and how badly he felt, he concentrated on the accident. And when he was able to stop thinking about that, he shifted his thoughts to where they should be—the place he intended to take Julie for their Friday evening date.

At four, he had an interview with a software supplier, then finished the day with a thirty-minute meeting involving two of his subs, both of whom had just returned from a symposium in Tallahassee.

Once Mildred had finished putting everything onto their software, he decided it was time to call it a day.

Just as he came out of his office and headed for the front door, Mildred looked up from her laptop. "Did you hear about that horrible accident on Semoran?"

He stopped dead in his tracks. His first reaction, of course, was to feel guilty for not telling her. He wanted to get angry with her for asking, because it made him feel uncomfortable. He knew it wasn't Mildred's fault; it was just that he'd been moderately successful at keeping his mind distracted from it and hadn't wanted to start obsessing about it all over again. And he certainly didn't want to engage in a lengthy discussion about it in the office.

"Why do you ask?" he managed.

"From what I saw on the local news, it was a doozy. There was even a taxi that had been involved. They said the taxi had come directly from the airport."

"So…?"

"I just thought it was a coincidence."

"How?"

"You came from the airport at roughly the same time."

"Small world, I guess."

"They showed a short clip of it on the news."

Robert didn't reply. He dreaded what was coming and didn't have any idea how he could talk his way out of this.

"They showed three people standing near the taxi, talking to a cop."

He waited tensely for her to continue.

She shot him a glare. "Why didn't you tell me you were involved?"

"I wasn't *involved*. I just happened to be in the cab when it happened."

"The journalist said the Camaro missed your cab by *inches*!"

"It missed us by at least a foot."

She sighed heavily. "Oh, Robert…"

Her tone made him feel like a kid who'd just been caught doing something stupid.

"I'm alive, all right? Look at me." He did a full three-sixty. "I'm standing right here. In the flesh. No wounds, cuts, or holes anywhere. Not a drop of blood showing—not that I can see. I'm talking to you, and I think I'm even making sense while I'm doing it. That couldn't happen with a concussion or brain injury, could it?"

"You really should've told me, you know…"

"Nothing to tell. We all survived. Anyway, you've been busy and so have I. Just forget about it, okay?"

He waited for a reply, but Mildred just sat there silently, glaring and looking hurt at the same time.

He shrugged, waved, and turned for the door.

Just before he pushed it open, she said, "Anyway, I'm glad you were able to get back safe and sound. And I'm really and truly very happy you weren't hurt."

"So am I. Thanks." He opened the door.

"Don't forget that nine a.m. call you've got tomorrow with Shimmerman Electronics."

"I won't."

Chapter 5

Julie's thoughts centered on Robert all afternoon and remained there as she pulled the day's revenues from the register and took them to her office.

While Gwen tidied up the floor and window displays, Julie placed the proceeds in the office safe, shut and secured the door, then went back to her desk to finish up the day's tallies on her laptop.

She began thinking of Robert once again, focusing on their encounter at the airport before moving on to their taxi ride. However, her thoughts, as if on cue, automatically shifted right back to the accident on Semoran.

She couldn't ignore the expression on Robert's handsome face when the three of them shook themselves out of their shock and waited patiently for their brains to try processing what had just happened. The mixture of confusion and fear—two qualities she had seen more times than she cared to remember—showed prominently on his face.

Robert was special. She knew that the moment they first met. His humility, combined with his looks and his concern for her safety, had been more than enough to convince her that he was indeed someone she wanted to get to know.

She had known many guys in her young life and had learned through painful experience that the special ones were few and far between. There were nice ones and good ones. There were those who had the capacity to be good but, unfortunately, came with too much baggage. There were even those who had once been good but had been damaged from life's struggles or a previous horrible relationship and would never be as they once were.

The warm, sensual feeling she experienced with Robert had been something she'd only read about in romance novels. He was soft-spoken, polite, great-looking, a good dresser, and possessed a terrific sense of humor. He was also very humble and caring—two things she hadn't seen much at all in the last few years.

The man was the complete package.

Careful, girl. You don't want to start believing what Jane had been saying since her divorce and right after your breakup with Nolan after eight months of what you had always thought was "actual bliss."

Coming to grips with reality after finding out the truth about Nolan had been extremely difficult. Her discovery that he was addicted to gambling. And drinking. And had a special fondness for blondes—especially when they were dancing around a pole. And when she discovered that he had been a longtime member and aficionado of one of those sleazy S&M clubs on the Trail, she realized that what they once had was not exactly what could be considered a match made in Heaven.

"Guys are just guys," her sister Jane kept telling her. "There are good ones and bad ones, and none of them come with a money-back guarantee. And not one of them I've ever known has ever looked back even once after deciding to shift with the tides and search for greener pastures."

Julie never wanted to think that way. She had always thought—hoped, actually—that a special kind of guy was out there, somewhere, and was just as lonely as she was. And if she were lucky, he could be looking for her. He would be a nice, sweet guy she could talk to. And listen to. And trust. And love with all her heart.

She knew to tread lightly. And slowly. And carefully. Robert wasn't married—at least, he'd *said* he wasn't. She had no idea if that was the truth, but she strongly sensed that he wasn't the type who would lie to her. She also had a very strong feeling that Bob was a man of his word. An honest man. With principles.

A man she could easily fall in love with and stay in love with for the rest of her life.

The problem here, of course, was his personal view of what had happened earlier, when she'd prevented the runaway Camaro from killing the three of them. If he'd accept what had happened. More importantly, if he'd accept her for doing what she'd done to prevent it.

But what could prove even more difficult was what she would tell him when he asked.

She sincerely hoped he would believe her.

***

Robert got back to the apartment just after six and went straight to the liquor cabinet to pour a small glass of bourbon.

He brought the bottle into the kitchen, sat down at the table, and poured two inches into a clean glass. He took a sip of the drink. As the fiery whiskey eased down his throat, he leaned back and sighed when he felt the knots loosening in his neck and back. It wasn't the workday that had his nerves all twisted up and pulled tight, it was the accident.

His mind went right back to it, just as it had more than a dozen times earlier that day.

"...Park Avenue," from the cabby.

Julie's eyes grew. She looked like she was getting ready to scream.

Then: *Stop the car!*"

Robert was knocked forward, his forehead slamming into the headrest.

Then: distant screams.

Reality returned, and he discovered that he was sitting in his kitchen, staring blankly at the rear window.

Sighing tiredly, he finished his drink, got up, and poured more from the bottle. He leaned against the counter and wondered how Julie had known what was about to happen.

Did she know? Or was he just imagining this?

She knew. He had no idea how, but he strongly suspected that she did.

Julie was somehow aware of what was about to happen, and because of this, the three of them were still alive.

So why was this bothering him?

Was it because her super sharp reflexes had gotten them out of what certainly would have been a fatal accident?

Or was it because she had done what he would have wanted to do, had he seen what was about to happen and been able to react as quickly as she had?

That was it, wasn't it?

It was the envy thing all along. After all, he was supposed to be the Alpha Guy. The Dude. Mr. Dominance. The Protector. The Hero. Mr. Man.

But he wasn't *any* of those things. He was merely the pathetic schmuck sitting in the back seat like a vegetable, while Julie, the fragile, helpless female, turned out to be the one who had saved the day.

That was the issue in a nutshell. He was the man in the equation. He was the one who was supposed to know how to react immediately—the one who should have been able to leap into action and literally morph into Superman.

But instead of celebrating the fact that he was still alive through the tremendously quick reflexes of a woman, he was questioning his manhood while quietly cursing Julie for doing what he would have been expected to do, if he'd possessed the reflexes necessary for such a heroic action.

Stop the whining!

Yes. He needed to do just that.

He also needed to forget his manly pride and remind himself that the stunning creature who had saved him from death was also the lady he was going to have dinner with, and that he needed to swallow his pride, accept what had happened, and let nature take its course.

That wasn't *too* much of a bitter taste to swallow, was it?

He suddenly had the urge to talk to Julie. To hear her voice. And, most of all, to remind himself just how lucky he had been, running into her in the first place.

A strange sense of genuine relief washed through him as he reached into his pocket and pulled out his cellphone.

***

Julie was about to fix dinner when her cell buzzed.

Hoping it was Robert, she rushed over to the counter and snatched it up.

The display read: *Robert*.

Smiling, Julie went over to the breakfast nook and sat. She'd wanted to call him earlier but didn't think that would be such a good idea. After all, she'd just met the man. Nowadays, women frequently took the initiative and did whatever they pleased, but even so, she didn't want to appear too eager.

Besides, Robert ran a software company. She didn't want to call him at the wrong time, inadvertently disrupting an important meeting, or some other issue he might be involved with.

Since it was now past six, she assumed he was probably calling from home.

"Hi."

"How're you doing?"

"Fine. How about you? You haven't bumped into anyone else, have you?"

Silence. Then laughter.

"You're not gonna let me live that one down, are ya?"

"I'm trying really hard not to."

"And doing a fine job of it, I might add."

"Thank you."

He groaned. "That wasn't supposed to be a compliment, ya know."

"I know. But thanks, anyway."

A brief pause. "I've been thinking about you all day."

"Really?"

"Definitely."

She laughed. "You've really been thinking about me all day? While you're trying to run a company? I honestly don't think that would be very productive. Do you?"

"Well, *not quite* all day, if you want to get technical. I do have distractions, you know. Business meetings. Conference calls."

"Did you have many of those?"

"Too many."

"I'm sorry."

"It's my fault, entirely."

"Well, since you're the one running the company, it's probably a good thing you're busy."

"Normally, yes."

"Normally?"

"Without those other pesky distractions."

"Like me?"

He paused. "Who else could we be talking about?"

"Now you've made me feel guilty."

"Sorry. But since it's all over now, we get to talk about fun stuff."

"You mean, like where you're gonna take me?"

"You're talking about tomorrow night?"

"That was the plan, wasn't it?"

"I guess it was, now that you've brought it up."

"You're not considering changing things on me, are ya?"

"Now why would I do that?"

"Who knows what you CEO guys do when you're conference-calling people?"

"It's called a conference call for a reason, you know. And that reason almost always involves company business. In other words, no fun stuff involved."

"I don't get many of those at the flower shop."

"You're lucky."

"I guess I am, now that I know how boring and unfun they are."

"Getting back to dinner… Have you ever been to Charlie's Steak & Seafood on Michigan?"

"I don't believe so. Is it a nice place?"

"Great food, terrific service, romantic atmosphere. What's *that* tell you?"

"It tells me you're probably planning to take me there."

"Can't fool you, can I?"

"Not yet..."

"What's *that* mean?"

"Doesn't a guy have to know the girl a little better before he starts messing with her mind?"

"I wouldn't know about *that*…"

"Are you sure?"

"I think I'd definitely remember messing with a girl's mind."

"Not if you're not really aware you're doing it when you're doing it…"

"How could I possibly do it without knowing I'm doing it?"

"You've already done it…"

"How?"

"How do you think?"

He groaned. "To be perfectly, honest, *you're* the one messing with *my* mind."

"How have I done *that*?"

"Well, for one thing, you got me hooked after just twenty minutes."

"Are you referring to the airport? Or our cab ride?"

"Definitely."

She hoped he wouldn't bring up the accident. "Actually, you did quite a number on me, too."

"I'm kinda glad. I'd hate to fall for a girl who wasn't giving me some cooperation in return."

"No need to worry about *that*."

"I'm *so* relieved."

"What about that other item you were talking about?"

"Which item is that?"

"I sorta got the idea that you were talking about more than one messing-with-your-mind thing."

"Oh, that."

"Care to elaborate?"

"Not much to say. Just that you saved my life."

There. Now it was out. But he hadn't sounded cruel or angry when he'd said it, so she had to assume it wasn't bothering him nearly as much as she'd thought.

This made her feel much better.

"Actually, it—"

"You're not gonna say, "it was nothing," are ya?"

She pressed her lips together and struggled to think of a different punchline.

"Because if you were, I was all set to be offended and humiliated."

"Please don't be. And I'm sorry if I did anything that made you feel—"

"Uncomfortable? Put out? Emasculated? Impotent? Any of those?"

She didn't reply. He still didn't sound angry, but he wouldn't have mentioned this if it hadn't been on his mind. But since she couldn't see his face, she wasn't sure about his feelings and decided not to say anything. But at least she hadn't sensed any resentment.

"Julie?"

Her pulse quickened. "Yes?"

"Because of you, we're all still here. The cabby, me, and you. Not only are we still here, but none of us was hurt. You did good. Don't ever think otherwise."

She smiled in relief.

"Don't tell me you were *worried*…"

"All right. I won't, then."

"You *were* worried?"

"You told me not to tell you."

"But you *were*, weren't you?"

"Well…"

"Why?"

"Actually, this same thing has happened to me before."

"People have taken issue with you just because you've got a nifty little second sight thingy going on in that gorgeous melon?"

She really didn't want to go into it. It was enough for her that her gift obviously didn't faze him. She didn't want to ruin a good thing.

"Some people," she said softly. "You know the drill."

"Yeah. I know all about people."

She just sighed.

"How long have you had this gift?"

"Since I was little." She hoped he wouldn't do what most of the others had done by asking her to go with them to the gambling casinos.

"It couldn't have been comfortable for you," he said. "When you were a kid, I mean."

"You're so right. But how did you know?"

"I was a kid once. Kids are assholes."

She laughed.

"It's true, isn't it?"

"You're certainly right about that."

"They pick on everyone for just about anything, so picking on someone for having special gift wouldn't be much of a stretch, would it?"

"They didn't pick on me for my gift," she said.

"But they did pick on you, didn't they?"

"They sure did."

"Why?"

"I had big feet."

They both laughed.

DAY TWO

Chapter 6

The next day, Robert's workday moved along smoothly, until just a few minutes before noon.

The latest conference call took much longer than it should have. Since there were eight people joining in on the call, including Andrew Sandusky, Robert's partner in the company, much of the meeting was spent trying to diffuse the occasional argument as well as keeping the confusion to a minimum.

Robert disliked conference calls but realized that in a functioning business dependent on outside sources, they were a necessary evil. Nevertheless, the event resulted in a modestly productive endeavor, and Robert was very relieved once it finished.

However, he soon found his relief short-lived when Don Vega, a Miami rep, caught him in the hall just moments after he'd left the conference room.

"That was you I saw on YouTube, wasn't it? It happened on Semoran, right? That double fatality with the red Camaro and the silver SUV?"

Vega was about thirty, dark-haired, good-looking, and very dapper in his dark blue, single-breasted, Italian-made suit. Representing Tekk-Biz, headquartered in Miami, Vega had been in Orlando the last two days dealing with T&S reps supervising future dealings with T&S and SKB Bits out of Tampa. Vega was soft-spoken and polite, but ruthless during meetings, and had a nasty habit of asking a lot of questions.

This discussion was something Robert didn't want to get involved in. He knew that if he acted even mildly evasive, Vega would consider it a red flag issue and hold on like a dog with a bone.

"You saw the whole thing?" he asked uneasily.

"There were six different videos covering it." Vega shrugged. "I was working my laptop and decided to do a little local surfing. I have relatives in the Central Florida area, so…"

"I was coming from the airport—"

"Semoran's kinda out of the way, isn't it? From Maguire, I mean."

This was going to be more difficult than he thought. "You certainly know the area pretty well…"

"As I just said, family…" Another shrug.

"The cabby picked up two of us, and we decided to drop her off first."

"You mean that tall, hot brunette babe standing beside you?"

Robert forced himself not to show any negative reaction. He knew how easy it would be to give himself away with the wrong expression. He hadn't cared for Vega calling Julie "babe" but knew better than voice any disapproval. Vega obviously didn't need much to get him sniffing around. "We were about a block or so from her stop when it happened."

"Where'd you meet her? At the airport? She's definitely primo stuff."

Robert struggled to keep from glaring. "She was very nice."

"Nice?" Vega shook his head. "That babe was *sweet*! I mean totally first-class and—"

"I'm kind of rushed right now." Robert made a show of pulling up his sleeve to sneak a peek at his watch.

Vega nodded but didn't miss a beat. "Looked like the Camaro had been close enough to peel a layer or two of paint right off the cab."

"One of the videos *showed* it happen?"

"Apparently someone was right there and caught the whole thing on their phone."

"Wonderful." Robert was not amused.

"What made the cabby stop? The report said the Camaro plowed through red without missing a beat. This meant you had the green, right?"

"Yeah."

"What happened? I know cabbies. They don't like to stop—not even for red lights. This one looked like he'd just stopped dead at about the same time the Camaro soared through."

"As I said, we were just lucky."

"You sure about that?"

It was getting more difficult to stay calm. "Whaddya mean?"

"If the cab had gone another foot, they would've spent the rest of the day scraping you, the babe, and the cabby off the pavement with a putty knife."

"I guess it just wasn't our time to go…"

"That's basically what your cabby said."

Robert blinked. "How the hell—"

"On YouTube."

"You mean—"

"Someone found him later on and asked him a few questions."

"Lucky me…"

"A *real* stroke of luck, wasn't it?" Vega apparently hadn't caught Robert's sarcasm.

"Yeah, I'm grateful we were able to stop in time."

"I don't mean *that*." Vega gave him a sly grin. "I meant, having a babe like that in the cab with you. Seemed like someone else was looking out for her." He pointed to the ceiling. "Lucky for you, too, eh, since you were right there with her?"

"Yep, luck seems to be oozing through my pores…" Robert turned abruptly and headed for his office.

"I'm still peeved at you," Mildred said softly, her trimmed brows mashed together.

He spun around and shot her a glare before realizing it. "I didn't know you thought so much about Vega's feelings."

"Vega? I don't care about him…"

"That sounds cold, Mil."

A glare. "You know exactly what I'm referring to."

"Not really, but I'm sure you're about to be extremely helpful."

"That accident you lied to me about."

"I wasn't in any accident. I've already told you about that. And I didn't *lie*."

56

"You didn't tell me. You know what they say about omission, don'tcha?"

"Unfortunately."

Her look was enough. He knew he had to give her some sort of explanation or the rest of the afternoon would not go well.

"I wasn't *in* that accident, Mil. Had things been just a little different, we *might* have been, but it just didn't happen that way."

"That's a very strange—and disturbing—way of putting it."

"It's what happened."

"You're making it sound almost as if you *wanted* to be involved."

"Now why would I want to be involved in a traffic fatality?"

"I don't know, but that's what you seem to be implying."

"All right, then. I'll say it a little differently this time. Here goes... I'm really and truly all sorts of glad, relieved, ecstatic, grateful, and tickled pink that I wasn't killed or placed in Intensive Care. I'm even relieved and giddy that the lady with me and the cabby were also not killed or placed in Intensive Care. Is that better?"

Another glare.

"Still not good enough?"

"Robert..." Mildred shook her head. "When I saw that clip on YouTube, my heart almost stopped."

"Really?"

"Yes."

"Have you seen a doctor about that?"

She closed her eyes and groaned.

"I'm all right. Shouldn't that be enough?"

"It really hurt my feelings that you didn't tell me. It makes me feel like you don't trust me. We've been together several years. I should think that our relationship has fashioned a definite trust as well as a strong business friendship."

"How does not telling you everything happening in my life translate into my not trusting you?"

"I would have appreciated knowing about it…"

"Would it help if I told you the next time it happens?"

"Now you're being ridiculous."

"Now you know what I think of this conversation." He turned and went into his office.

***

Robert spent the rest of the afternoon trying to forget what Mildred had said.

"It really hurt my feelings that you didn't tell me. It makes me feel like you don't trust me."

But what Vega said

("someone else was looking out for her")

had freaked him out even more.

And when he watched the five-minute video using his laptop, his pulse hastened, and the back of his neck grew hot.

The short, thirty-second interview with the cab driver made the situation even worse.

Cabby: "I had to change my shorts when that damn Camaro roared past!"

Interviewer (a slender, young black-haired woman in a maroon jogging outfit): "How did you know to stop when you did? You were, after all, proceeding on green, weren'tcha? You had the right of way. If you'd kept on going—"

"If I'd kept on goin'," the cabby said, chuckling, "all three of us woulda been red stains smeared all over the fuckin' pavement!"

Robert sighed tiredly and let his head fall back. He closed his eyes. His thoughts ran wild, and he found himself once again at a complete loss. But when his mind finally settled down, what he came up with was something that had occurred to him before. And, like it or not, he realized that it was quite possibly the only thing he needed to consider that would put an end to this fruitless battle raging in his head.

He was still alive. It didn't matter how or why fate had turned its cold, dark glare in his direction. Because of the lightning-quick actions of a young woman, he was alive and well, and ready to fight another day.

But even though he had just found peace with himself and what happened, he couldn't help wondering if this was enough for him to think that his budding relationship with the young woman who had saved his life would be able to progress naturally.

***

At 3:30, Carlo Baroni's phone rang.

It was Joan, his secretary. "It's someone calling himself Johnny, sir."

Carlo sat back in his seat and frowned. "He didn't give ya his last name?"

"I believe he said Ashland. Should I insist on more information? Or should I just tell him—"

"He say why he's callin'?"

"He said he discovered something you'd probably be interested in."

He grunted. "I'm interested in a lot of things. He say what, exactly?"

"He said he'd like to discuss it with you…"

Carlo cursed under his breath. *Some stronzone calling himself Johnny Ashland, who knows something I'll be interested in, and the bastard only wants to talk to me. Terrific.*

But he knew he had to find out what it was.

"Switch him over."

Carlo sipped some port wine and sat back in his chair.

The name Ashland didn't exactly ring a bell. It sounded a *little* familiar, but nothing that actually jumped out at him…

Hell, he knew a shitload of Johnny's. In fact, everyone he could think of knew a shitload of Johnny's. Carlo's brother's name was Johnny. So was his brother-in-law. His lawyer's name was John, as well as one of the bouncers in his strip club, Club Venus. The manager of the club itself, who had managed one of his hot spots in Miami just a few years back, was named Johnny.

Maybe he should have told Joan to get more information after all.

But it wasn't necessary. He knew how to hang up on people. And if this dude turned nasty or started making threats, Carlo knew how to handle that as well.

You don't become the most successful club owner in Central Florida by being a nice guy. And you sure as hell don't get anywhere by letting assholes walk all over you.

Click.

"Mr. Baroni?"

"Who's this?"

"I'm Johnny Ashland, sir."

It sounded like a kid. Mid-twenties, maybe...

He sat back and tried once again putting a face to the name. It didn't ring a bell. "That name s'posed to mean somethin' to me?"

"You used my father's services about a year ago, sir."

"Ashland. Ashland." He tried a little harder. *Father's services. Insurance, maybe? Something else?* Just then, an image began forming in his head. "Sounds *vaguely* familiar... Refresh my memory."

"My dad's a private detective, sir. He—"

"Gotcha." The image instantly became clear. "He cleaned up a dirty little mess for me last September, I believe. This stripper I'd hired. She was doin' a number on one of my bouncers and it was impactin' the club. Lenny started comin' in drunk and I had to get rid of him. Damn shame. Lenny was a damn good bouncer. Your dad, he did a fine job for me. What's all this about? You got somethin' I need to hear?"

"Well, sir, I do legwork for my dad nowadays, and sometimes I come into contact with people who have dealt with you or your son."

"Go on..."

"I was talking to someone today about a traffic fatality that happened on North Semoran just the other day, and—"

"Heard about that one. Nasty."

"Yes, sir. Anyway, something about one of the vehicles involved in the accident sparked my memory. I did a little research and found out something about it."

"What about it?"

"The vehicle that caused the accident was a red Camaro, and it was apparently driven by someone who used to work at Club Venus."

He sat up in his seat. "How long ago?"

"I'm not really sure."

"Are we talkin' male or female here?"

"Female."

"Was she a dancer? Waitress?"

"I'm just going by the license plate, sir. It was taken off another vehicle, and that vehicle was stolen from one of the bouncers who used to work at your club. I haven't seen the girl's face. They haven't shown it on any of the news sources yet."

"Why should any of this interest me?"

"Well, as I just said, she was involved with one of your bouncers, and it looks like the Camaro she was driving belonged to your son."

Carlo remembered Frankie mentioning one of his cars being stolen. This happened a while ago. Frankie had been major pissed about it. "Frankie's had a bunch of cars. About a year ago, he told me someone made off with one of his Camaros. Ya tryin' to say this red one was his?"

"I'm pretty sure it was, sir. I recalled seeing a picture of it last year, and when I saw that accident on Semoran, it kinda hit home."

"What makes ya think it's the same car? When Frankie had it, it was a dark blue."

"The spoiler looks pretty much the same, sir. It's smashed up, but there was a nick on it that I'd seen in another picture. I'm almost certain it's the same car."

"Frankie was really pissed off when it was stolen. He loved that car."

"Well, if we can get the PIN from the police—"

"That's about all you'll be able to get. Judging by the shots I saw, the damn thing's trash."

"Yes, sir."

"The driver. The bitch died, right?"

"Yes, sir. They think cocaine was involved."

"So? She was a cokehead. Why should this matter?"

"From what I heard, she apparently got the stuff from someone working in your club."

"I run a clean club, dammit!" He hated when shit like that started up. People tended to grow giant ears and big mouths. To make things worse, the idiots also believed every word of it. And when the big guys got wind of it, they started flapping their lips, and before you knew it, it was all over the Internet. The phones started ringing and the elite parasites threatened all sorts of lawsuits and fines if the matter wasn't tended to and killed quickly, without any names leaking out. "I don't allow that shit in my club."

"Yes, sir."

"Is that it? You're pretty sure that was Frankie's Camaro?"

"Sir, if you don't mind, I'd like to come over and show you a few of the YouTube shots I've made of the car."

"Why?"

"Well, for one thing, it'll clear up any insurance claims."

"You've got good, clear shots of the car?"

"I managed to work up some fair closeups of the spoiler and the spinners. Apparently she didn't change much except for having the car painted. And the paint job wasn't first-rate."

"That'll work. Sounds like your daddy taught ya well."

"He tried his best, sir."

Chapter 7

At 4:00, Julie decided to take off work early to give herself extra time to prepare for her date with Robert.

She quickly found that she was totally confused. She didn't want to come off looking too classy and she didn't want to look drab, either. Or cheap. This would be her first date with a fabulous guy, and she wanted to impress him without embarrassing him or distracting him too much.

And this meant looking as attractive and as sexy as possible without appearing overeager, or desperate.

From what Robert had told her, the eatery he'd picked for their date enjoyed a solid reputation for great food and a romantic atmosphere. She decided that if Robert thought it special enough to take her there, then it must be terrific. She didn't think he would have selected one of those ritzy places patronized by the local elite. He just didn't seem that kind of guy.

She chose a long sleeve light blue blouse and a short—but not *too* short—black skirt, and open-toed black sandals with two-inch heels.

Her hair looked okay, but a careful once-over with the pick certainly wouldn't hurt. It wouldn't be very bright to overdo the hairspray, either. As a precaution, she performed a quick dusting. After checking herself out in the mirror, she decided that she looked presentable enough—at least, for her own taste.

She knew not to overstate the jewelry as well. The pearl necklace, given to her by her grandmother, as well as her favorite gold bracelet, onyx ring, tiny silver earlobe studs, and a silver pinkie ring would suffice.

It was 4:28 when her cell phone buzzed.

Julie smiled at the display.

"Everything okay?" she asked.

"I was gonna ask you the same thing."

"You remember how to get to my place, right?"

"Sure do."

"Then you should be here shortly."

"I'm already halfway there."

"Just halfway?"

"Traffic hasn't been cooperating much."

"It never does."

"I've been trying to communicate with everyone using my famous glare, but it hasn't been working."

"You must have your visor down."

"How'd you know?"

"What else could be hiding your famous glare?"

"If I push the visor up, the dazzling Central Florida sun will blind me, so my glare won't be nearly as effective."

"It wouldn't be much fun, stopping at the Mall to find you a walking stick before our date."

"It would be even *less* fun, picking you up and driving you to the restaurant while I'm blind."

She groaned. "I've have to read the menu to you and everything."

"Then I guess we wouldn't want any surprises, would we?"

She smiled. "Not *those* kind..."

"What kind are *you* talking about?"

"The kind we need to discuss in person."

"This isn't what I should be thinking about while I'm stuck in this heavy afternoon traffic. I do have to concentrate on other things right now, you know..."

"Be careful, now. I don't want you to have an accident."

"I don't want me to have one of those, either."

"Isn't it wonderful that we agree on so many things?"

Click.

She smiled and felt her pulse flutter at the same time.

Easy, girl. This might be a first date, but you've already spent some quality time with this guy and have decided he could very well be the one you end up spending the rest of your life with. He's easy to look at, even easier to talk to, and he doesn't think you're a freak for what you did in the cab. Now take a breath, square those shoulders, think sexy, and try very hard not to make a total mess of things...

***

"I can't possibly tell if that pile of twisted metal is my son's Camaro."

Carlo Baroni turned away from his laptop and shot a glare at   Johnny Ashland.

Being in Carlo Baroni's office had quickly become a frightening experience. The man was intimidating, to say the least. Six feet tall, at least

67

two hundred and fifty pounds, and his hands looked like a pair of flesh-covered chunks of stone. His eyes were large and very dark, his graying black hair thick and curly despite his age, and his loud, booming voice made Johnny's ears ring. The man had been running strip clubs in the Central Florida area for many years and had been able to take down all the competition, and without much trouble.

Johnny's father hadn't exaggerated when he'd said this man could turn a hardened gang member into a whimpering mass of Jell-O with just one glare.

And right now, the dude wanted answers.

Although Johnny realized the big man needed to know what was going on, he cursed himself once again for becoming directly involved. Right now, he was developing a renewed admiration for his father for dealing with him.

"I'm pretty sure it's the same car, sir," he said in a soft voice.

"How sure *are* ya?"

"As I told you, the spoiler seems identical to another picture I remember when I first saw the car."

"I need a better picture to make sure. These eyes"—he pointed to his face—"ain't as good as they once were, ya know."

"You mean you'd like a different angle?"

"Picture, angle—what the hell's the difference?"

"Well, sir, a picture—"

"I know what the hell a *picture* is, dammit!" The man's loud voice made the walls vibrate. "I look stupid to ya?"

Johnny told himself to keep his big mouth shut unless he was absolutely certain that what he might say wouldn't turn out to be a painful experience.

"You gonna help me out here? Or just sit there like an idiot?"

"I can find you a better angle, sir…"

"How, exactly?"

"I'll pull a shot from a zoom of the taxi the Camaro almost t-bonedf. The wreckage can clearly be seen once the cab is on the left side of the screen."

"All this was in the video?"

"Yes, sir."

Carlo Baroni shrugged his massive shoulders. "*I* didn't see it…"

"Actually, it's on a different video."

"When did *this* happen?"

"Not long after the cop cars got there and roped off the area."

Johnny could tell the big man was getting irritated. He just hoped Carlo wouldn't take his wrath out on him. The man's temper was legendary. It was also frightening. Carlo Baroni was known for a great many things, but one thing he never did, according to Johnny's father, was take prisoners. He destroyed them, and he did it as painfully as possible.

The big man was shaking his head.

"It's really easy to find, sir…"

"Why didn't *I* see it? I watched the whole damn thing on two different videos—"

"Someone else picked it up from their cell."

"From the same place?"

"This other person—a woman, I think it was—had just come out of the pharmacy about half a block southeast of the accident scene."

"And you say it shows the car better? Even though the damn thing was squished into the side of that SUV?"

"I'm pretty sure it does, sir."

"All right, then. Get on with this."

"It's not a problem, sir. You can find just three down from the list."

The big man clicked on it. It took him only two seconds to find the two-minute podcast.

The video showed the wreckage and the crowd wandering around, their cell phones waving at the scene, while three cops busily roped off the area.

"This is the same as the first one," he said irritably. "Just in a different place."

"Just wait, sir. It gets better."

The cab sat in the middle of the intersection. Three people stood a few feet from the driver's side, talking to a uniform, who was writing in his notebook. The cabby, a short, thickset Hispanic, was pointing at the wreckage as he spoke to the cop. The man and woman stood closer to the cab, near the rear door, both looking uncomfortable and nervous.

Johnny was certain the big man would be able to see the difference in this shot. This camera was positioned at least twenty feet closer to the cab than the original. It would show the details of the rear of the Camaro the big man needed to see.

The big man's thick brows bunched together, and his facial features became a tense mask. He groaned, then shook his head. "Dammit, I can't tell for sure. That damn brunette's head's in the way!"

"Sir? Maybe if I zoom in and—"

Carlo Baroni grunted and pulled out his cell. "You in the building?" he asked. "Or at Babes?"

Johnny heard Frank Baroni's voice say, "I'm at Babes, Pop. What's up?"

"Got somethin' you might be interested in. Busy right now?"

"Not really…"

"Then c'mon over to my office."

"Be there in five minutes."

***

Robert and Julie shared a window seat overlooking the palmetto-lined lake just down the slope from the rear of Charlie's Steakhouse.

The meal was excellent, the service top-rate, and the atmosphere soft and dreamlike, as in a romantic movie. The view of the lake just beyond the window, though blissfully peaceful, couldn't stop Robert from gazing endlessly at Julie.

He realized he was overdoing it. He even knew that he was making himself appear desperate. But he just couldn't help it. Julie was the most stunning woman he had ever known, and he kept resisting the urge to pinch himself to make sure this evening wasn't just one of those vivid dreams a man experiences only once or twice in his life.

But it wasn't merely her looks that had totally captivated him. Julie possessed a rare quality he had never known before. Although he couldn't exactly put his observation into words, he strongly felt that she could somehow sense what he was thinking. The incident in the cab had convinced him that Julie was more than just a beautiful woman. While he still found himself amazed by her ability to sense what was about to happen, he discovered that he felt intimidated by this skill. He knew he shouldn't feel this way. Many others—both male and female— possessed similar capabilities.

Robert finished his second glass of red wine and was surprised that he was able to do so without spilling it. Although the evening was turning out just great, he nonetheless found his insecurities making an unwelcome appearance. While he stared helplessly at Julie, he noticed that she'd been watching him as well. But instead of enjoying this, or considering it a great compliment, he found that it made him uncomfortable.

"Why do I have this funny feeling that you're waiting for me to do something?" he asked uneasily.

"Define something."

"How about another unfortunate mishap on my part based on our history?"

She blinked. "We have a *history*?"

"You've forgotten already?"

"History was never my strong point. And since I seem to have a slew of things going on up there in my brain right now, a complete refresh would help immensely."

"Our history involves my clumsiness. I'm sure you remember my unforgettable debut at the airport."

"I thought you would have chosen a better hobby by now."

"I kinda think this hobby chose *me*."

"Didn't you tell me you weren't gonna do stuff like that anymore?"

"I don't remember saying that…"

"You *should* have…"

"Well, the good thing is that I haven't done anything like that tonight, have I?"

"I never thought you would."

"Then why the stare?"

"You really need to ask?"

"What can I say? My clumsiness brought a bunch of insecurities right along with it."

"No need. I'm just admiring the view."

I just can't get over this. I really don't want to pinch myself. If this really is a dream, I don't want to know it, and I sure don't want it to end. Ever.

In the midst of his thoughts, he suddenly noticed that their waitress was standing beside him, smiling down at them.

"I'm sorry. I didn't see you standing there."

"Was everything all right?" she asked.

"Perfect." He realized once again that he was still gazing helplessly at Julie.

"Everything was great." Julie nodded. "Thank you."

The waitress placed the small metal tray on the table next to his elbow. The bill lay face-down in its center, beneath two mints. "I'll be back in a few moments." She turned to walk away.

"That won't be necessary." He pulled out his billfold, removed two hundreds and slipped them beneath the check. "That second one's for you. Also, what's left of the first one."

The waitress' smile beamed. "*Thank* you! And *please* come back!"

"If I can con this lovely lady into a second date, we'll definitely be back."

Outside, as they strolled arm-in-arm down the walk to the gravel lot, she said, "What makes you think I have to be conned?"

He stopped walking and once again found himself helplessly trapped inside the hypnotic pull of those beautiful eyes. Had he heard her correctly? Her smile was encouraging, but he still couldn't be sure. He'd known a lot of women and had learned quite a few things that proved common with most of them. They frequently sent out mixed signals, which told him that he should consider himself extremely fortunate if he ever met a girl who truly meant what she said. "Are you trying to say you won't?"

"What do you think?"

"I think I'm not quite sure."

She smiled. "*I* would be if I were you."

Once again, confusion overwhelmed him. Her expression appeared both serious and encouraging.

"You mean you won't *have* to be?"

"Are you surprised?"

"Well, yeah…"

"Why?"

"You seem, well, much too—"

74

"Too what?"

When he didn't respond right off, she said, "I'm here with you, right?"

"Yeah…"

"Then what's the problem?"

"I just thought—"

"You thought what?"

"I guess I thought that maybe the Universe had suffered a sudden glitch, and something totally against all odds slipped through it before anyone caught wind of it."

"Are you referring to our meeting one another?"

He nodded.

She laughed. "Robert Townsend, I do believe you can be an idiot."

"Julie Kenner, I do believe you're absolutely right."

"Know what else I believe?"

"What's that?"

"I believe you're a terrific kisser."

"But I haven't even tried to—"

Her warm, moist lips cut off the rest of his statement.

Moments later, when their kiss ended, she kept her face very close. Once again, he fully understood the hypnotic power in those eyes. They seemed to be pulling him into her aura. He felt warm in there. Content. And happier than he'd ever been.

Once his heart had slowed, he whispered, "What's the verdict?"

She smiled. "I think I'm gonna need to do quite a bit more research on that."

"Really? How much?"

"I'll let you know when I've finished."

He could feel his heart beginning to accelerate again.

"Now could you do us both a favor?" she asked.

"What is it?"

"Please take me back to my place so I can figure out if I'm right about that other thing."

He was afraid to ask. "*What* other thing?"

She tapped him lightly on the cheek. "I'll let *you* figure that one out, silly."

Chapter 8

The office door opened.

Frankie came in, closed the door, and marched right over. "Wanna see me, Pop?"

Carlo looked up from his laptop and gestured for his son to come closer. "Come over here. Take a look at this. Tell me whatcha see."

"Whaddya want me to see, Pop?"

"The kid, here, mighta just found what's left of your Camaro."

Frankie glanced at the kid, then turned back to Carlo. "What the hell happened?"

"The damn thing's wrecked, but he thinks it's your car. Tell me what *you* think."

Frankie moved closer and stood over Carlo. He bent and peered at the screen. A moment later, he stiffened, gasped, and straightened. "Shit!"

Carlo looked up at his son. "A real mess, ain't it?"

Frankie began shaking his head. He groaned.

"Insurance'll take care of it, don'tcha worry."

Frankie didn't say anything. His gaze seemed to be glued to the screen.

Carlo sat back in his seat. What the hell was going on? He stared at the laptop, studied the screen for a few moments, then turned back to Frankie. "The hell's wrong? You've got eight other classic cars in the garage. You lost this one nearly a year ago. What's got your panties in a wad?"

Frankie pulled in a huge gulp of air.

Carlo turned back to the screen. "We still talkin' about the car?"

Frank just continued to stare.

"Kid?"

No reply. This wasn't like Frankie *at all*.

"Kid, you're scarin' me…" Carlo focused on the three standing near the cab again. Nothing about the guy in the good suit should bother the kid. Nothing about the cabby, either. However, knowing his son as well as he did, Carlo knew this had to be about the brunette. Nothing else made sense.

Carlo did a zoom on the girl's face. He turned back to his son. "Care to tell me what's bummin' you out so much about this?"

Frankie didn't reply. His loose shrug made Carlo want to grind his teeth.

Carlo took a breath. *Easy, now…* "Wanna give me just a tad more info than that? That shrug just made you look like a schmuck."

Frankie's blank expression didn't clear up anything.

"Dammit, Frankie, what the hell is freakin' you out about this?"

The boy didn't reply.

"Frankie?"

His son sighed deeply.

"A sigh ain't cuttin' it, either. You know me by now. I'm blunt and to the point, and I don't care a fuckin' bit about any sorta bullshit. I was raised this way. I ask you a question? You answer. You don't answer? I think maybe somethin's wrong. I think somethin's wrong? We fix whatever the hell it is. It's that simple. *Capisc*?"

78

His son nodded.

"Good. Now…tell me what's goin' on. I know you, kid. You love babes. You're just like the old man. Now we're lookin' at one helluva babe, and you look like you just lost your nut. You gotta tell me about this babe so I know what to do next."

Frank sighed again, then glanced at the kid sitting on his right.

"This somethin' private?"

Frank nodded.

"Kid?" Carlo tossed the boy a wink. "Make tracks."

With a word, Johnny Ashland jumped up and hurried out of the room.

Carlo stared at his son, who had turned back to the laptop. Frankie had turned pale and was shaking. Carlo knew his son. The boy had nerves of steel. There wasn't that much that could shake him up this badly.

"Lemme take a stab at this," he said. "I gotta worry about this babe?"

After a long silence, Frankie nodded.

"You knock her up?"

"No, Pop…"

"She see somethin' she shouldn'ta seen? Heard somethin' she shouldn't've heard?"

A nod.

"This got anything to do with a recent problem?"

Another nod.

Carlo could feel his pulse sputter. If this was about what he suspected, the kid had really messed up. "Dammit, Frankie, this got somethin' to do with that Betz son of a bitch?"

"Yes, Pop."

Dammit all to hell!

"She *saw* somethin'?"

A nod.

"In other words, we're both lookin' at a dead girl?"

"Yes, Pop…"

"She ain't dead, is she?"

"No, Pop."

"She's s'posed to be, but she ain't. She ain't, 'cause she's standin' right there, bigger than shit, gettin' in a cab, and you can't do any of that shit when you're dead. Yes?"

Frankie nodded.

"You tellin' me you didn't take care of this when you were s'posed to?"

"I *thought* I did, Pop…"

"If you did what you were s'posed to do, we wouldn't be seein' her gettin' in a cab right now, would we?"

His son couldn't take his eyes off the screen.

"Well?"

"I guess not…"

"Know what I'm thinkin', don'tcha?"

Frankie didn't respond. His eyes remained glued to the screen.

"You're tellin' me you gave this to someone else?"

His son nodded.

"Why the hell didn'tcha handle it yourself?"

Frankie lowered his face and stared at the carpet.

"What the hell have I been tellin' you all your damn life about shit like this?"

Frankie sighed.

"That's no answer and you know it."

Frankie shook his head. "Take care of things yourself so...so—"

"So you don't have to worry if they were done right. The way things are nowadays? You gotta be helluva lot more diligent now. Folks are shitheads. They're stupid and unreliable, and you just can't trust 'em. Remember that?"

"Yes, sir."

"Now...tell me what you gotta do."

Frankie groaned. "I know what I gotta do."

"This mean you're gonna take care of it yourself?"

"Damn right it does!"

"Good. Now go do it. But this time, do it right!"

Without another word, Frankie hurried out of the room.

***

Bill Torchia couldn't ignore the heavy feeling settling in his gut as he hurried down the hall, where Frank Baroni's office sat at the far end.

Frank was an okay guy to work for. But even so, he was a hard-headed Italian from New York and had been molded and trained by his daddy, Carlo, whose dominance had been developed through many years of Mob influence.

Frank was not at all what anyone could call the laid-back type. His hair-trigger temper defined him, and he held on to a grudge like a tick on a dog. He was the best guy to have in your corner when you were doing things the way he wanted them done, but if you fucked up or decided to do the job a different way, you'd find it much safer in the long run to pull up stakes immediately and find a new life in a secluded place a thousand miles away from the state of Florida.

This sinking feeling weighing him down began with the phone call he'd received from Frank just five minutes earlier. The big dude sounded seriously pissed about something but hadn't gone into detail. Bill's mind looped as he made the trip down the long, carpeted hall, trying to remember if he had messed up or forgotten to do anything in the last few days. His memory pulled up nothing, and he found himself at as much of a loss now as when Frank had called and angrily ordered Bill to get his ass to his office, pronto.

Being a bouncer at one of Carlo's clubs had never been very demanding for Bill. At six-three and two-twenty, he had propelled his name high up in the MMA ranks just a few years back, retiring undefeated after more than thirty professional fights in just two years. He was now thirty-seven, had been a bouncer for the last four years, and never had any trouble with any of his bosses. Carlo, the big man, always stayed in the background and made his suggestions known to his next in line—which, in this case, was his son Frank. Frank, on the other hand, had no qualms about bullying his boys, believing this technique encouraged loyalty through fear. Frank believed, possibly through practical experience, that fear was quite possibly the most effective way of obtaining the best results.

But whatever had pissed off Frank so much had Bill stumped. His first reaction had been to ask what was going on, but the man's tone strongly suggested that he kept his mouth shut. Bill had known and worked with hard-headed Italians for several years and could easily read the danger signs. And he instinctively knew when to step forward as well as when to shut up and do as he was told.

That phone call clearly told him that his mouth should stay closed tightly until Frank asked him something. It also told him that whatever he said should not leave his throat unless he was absolutely sure that what he would say would not get him fired.

Taking a deep breath, he stepped up to the door and knocked.

"C'mon in," came the muffled reply.

Bill opened the door, slipped into the room, and closed the door behind him. One look at the harsh glare on his boss' dark, rough-featured face made him groan, and the heaviness in his gut rapidly turned into a dull, throbbing ache.

***

Julie lay beside Robert, watching him intently.

She never thought she could find someone like him and couldn't help wondering if any of this truly happened. That awkward but wonderful encounter at the airport? The taxi ride? The close call on

Semoran? The beautiful candlelight dinner overlooking the lake?

Was *any* of this real?

Or was it something she'd always imagined true love would be in a perfect world?

She had learned from a very young age that this world was far from perfect. Knowing this, she also realized nothing she had experienced before in her life could compare to what she was feeling right this very moment, as she lay beside him.

Nothing could compare to the last couple of hours. Nothing in the world could ever change the outcome of the wonderful evening she had just shared with this lovely man.

Her parents divorced when she was just twelve years old. Since many of her friends and relatives were also divorced, separated, or had never been engaged or married, she had never really known anyone other than her grandparents who had spent their lives being happily married.

Robert seemed to be thinking along the same lines. As he lay beside her, he also wondered if the evening had been real. If he was falling in love with Julie. If they had even the slightest chance of being happy together in this strange and confusing high-tech world of social media and brief, casual, one-dimensional relationships. If he could honestly make her as happy as he thought she should be.

She knew he was thinking these thoughts because she was able to sense them—just as she could sense much of everything else. Sensing them just as her grandmother had done all those many years ago, when the sweet old lady was living alone in her large farmhouse just a few miles from Moundsville, West Virginia, where she lived out her final years tending to her flowers and keeping the birds and the butterflies fed and happy.

Julie fondly remembered that one summer the family had visited her grandmother the year Julie had turned ten and discovered some things about herself that didn't make much sense. It was the time she had first asked her grandmother what was so different about her and why her friends thought her weird.

Mom and Dad were still married at that time. They lived just a few miles from Columbus, in Westerville, and would continue living there until business pressures began changing Dad, turning him cold and ruthless and nervous, causing him and Mom to drift apart, until they both decided to go their separate ways.

Julie and her older sister Janie stayed with Mom. Just a few months after Mom and Dad divorced, the three of them moved to Winter Park, where Mom's sister had been living. Julie hated moving so far away from Gram, who was her very best friend, and was devastated when the wonderful old lady died last year. But Julie would always feel good about herself, knowing that she never failed to call her special friend at least twice every month, and always managed to save up enough money each year to make a pilgrimage to see the sweet lady and enjoy her wonderful company up until her death.

The last time they'd visited Gram as a family was that last summer Dad and Mom had spent their vacation together. Julie fondly remembered that lovely summer afternoon when she and her grandmother strolled down the grassy path near the pine forest behind the farmhouse, where birds and butterflies flitted and hopped from every tree and flower.

This was the very first time her grandmother told her about "the gift" the sweet lady had been blessed with all her life. It was the very same gift that was somehow passed down to Julie, who first noticed it when she and a few of her neighborhood friends were playing one Saturday morning, the first week after school was out.

"We were about to cross the street," Julie told Gram, "when I had this strange feeling we should stay right where we were."

"What sort of feeling was it, child?" Gram asked.

"It was really hard to explain."

"Did it scare ya?"

"Not *scare*, exactly. Just kinda, well, worried me."

"Did you feel a kind of darkness coming on? A heavy warmth rubbing against you?"

"*That's* what it was, I think. A darkness. And a warmth. Almost like I could feel a storm coming."

"Anything else, child?"

"I dunno. I didn't hear any traffic, so it wasn't that. I just thought we should wait a little while before we crossed the street."

"And you did, didn'tcha?"

"Yes, ma'am."

"How'd you keep your friends from crossing?"

"I told them a little white lie."

86

"What was it?"

"I told them I saw something weird in the grass, and they came right over to see what it was."

"What happened then?"

"A truck raced by just as Cindy turned around and came back to where the rest of us were standing."

Gram smiled. Julie could tell the old lady knew exactly what happened. But just as she was about to ask her grandmother about it, the old woman patted her gently on the shoulder. "You've got it, child."

Julie didn't understand what the old lady had just said. "W-What have I got?"

"The gift."

"Huh?"

The old woman nodded. "Just like me. I've had it nearly all my life."

"Really? You mean, sort of like—"

"Like an extra sense, child. Some call it a sixth sense. Others call it a premonition while still others call it somethin' else. There are a hundred different names for it, but it all boils down to this: you've got this feeling that someone's always looking out for you."

"When did you first notice it?"

"I was about your age, I guess. That makes it about seventy years, give or take a month or two."

"You've had it that long?"

The old woman nodded. "And each year, it seems stronger than ever."

"What exactly *is* this…this gift? I mean, do you have any idea how it found…how I got—"

"Hi…" Robert had turned on his side and was smiling at her.

"Hi."

He reached over with his free hand and gently brushed some hair away from her cheek. "You feeling okay?"

She sighed. "*Way* more than just okay. How about you?"

"Never better. You seemed deep in thought. What were you thinking about?"

She opened her mouth and suddenly realized she couldn't remember. All she seemed to care about was this terrific guy's smile. And the way he was looking at her. And, of course, how warm and content his beautiful chestnut eyes were making her feel. She just shrugged.

"I guess it's not important, is it?"

She smiled at his closeness. His smile—as well as his touch and the heat coming from him—told her he wanted to go at it again. "Not nearly as important as what I'm thinking now."

"Is it the same thing I'm thinking?"

"I'll bet it's the *very* same thing."

His face wrinkled. "Why do I think you know exactly what's going on inside my head?"

"Because it's probably the very same thing that's going on inside mine."

As he moved his face closer, she wrapped her arms around his neck and pressed her lips against his.

***

Frank Baroni's glare chilled Bill Torchia to the bone.

Bill found that he couldn't move. He stayed right where he was, his muscular back pressed firmly against the door. Frank's expression intimidated him, and Bill had no intention of taking a single step farther into the room until it was absolutely necessary.

This meant he wouldn't budge unless Frank actually—

"Get over here and *sit down*."

This is it. I've got to do this.

Forcing himself not to trip or stumble, Bill crossed the room in the same manner as a prisoner facing a firing squad. He had no idea why he was feeling so guilty, but the searing gaze emanating from Frank Baroni's wild, deep-set eyes gave him no choice. Frank was clearly pissed at him. Bill just hoped his boss was wrong about whatever it was.

Bill reached the desk and stopped behind the chair. He knew he was supposed to sit down; he just didn't want to. He felt much safer behind the chair. He needed some sort of shield and decided the chair would suffice. He feared that if he did circle the chair and lower his butt into it, he'd provide Frank with the perfect target.

Thinking these thoughts suddenly made him intensely angry with himself. He was as strong as an ox, younger, and in much better shape than Frank, who wolfed down lasagna and porterhouse steaks with his double vodka martinis. Bill had been a mixed martial arts champion for more than three years, for God's sakes.

In other words, he bowed to no one…

But right now, he felt like a rabbit trapped in a cage with an enraged mongoose.

"Siddown, dammit."

Swallowing a sizeable lump, Frank slowly circled the chair and sat.

"Wonderin' why you're here?"

Bill nodded.

"You're here for one reason and one reason only. Wanna know what that reason is?"

Again, he nodded.

"You fucked up, plain and simple."

Bill waited for the man to continue. He suspected things would go much better if he spoke only when he was told to.

"Know *how* you fucked up?"

Bill shook his head.

"Know *why*?"

Bill shook his head once again.

Frank clicked his keyboard and turned it around so the screen faced Bill. "Have a look. And try real hard not to feel like a total moron."

The screen showed a YouTube video of a cab with three people standing beside it. They were talking to a cop, who was making notes in a thick black book. In the background, firefighters were busy getting debris off the street, three other cops were directing traffic and pushing the crowd back, and several paramedics were placing two covered bodies on two gurneys in front of what looked like the wreckage Bill had heard about a couple of days ago.

"Look familiar?" Frank asked.

"That happened on Semoran, right?"

"Right on the button."

"Some babe—a stripper, I think—slammed into an SUV. Both died, right?"

"The babe was drivin' a red Camaro. Recognize it?"

"Not from that angle…"

"It belonged to me."

"Really?" Bill remembered Frank once having a big-block blue Camaro. "That's—that was *your* ride?"

"For a while. Till someone decided to piss me off by stealin' it."

"I remember." Bill had heard that one of the girls had a problem with coke and took to selling herself for fixes. Frank heard about this and fired her not too long before his Camaro turned up missing. Bill wondered if she'd been the one who'd stolen it. He just couldn't see what any of this had to do with him.

Frank turned the screen to face him and began clicking again. About half a minute later, he turned it back around.

This time, the video showed a closeup of the threesome standing in front of the driver's door of the cab. One was the cabby, the other, a clean-shaven guy in a good suit. The third, a shapely, good-looking brunette babe with fabulous legs who looked eerily familiar…

"Recognize her?"

Bill leaned forward in his seat and squinted.

Just then, Frank zoomed in on her face. "This help any?"

Bill's jaw dropped as the image registered in his brain.

"How 'bout now? Ring-a-ding ding?"

Clenching his teeth, Bill cringed in his seat.

Frank sat back and glared. "I take it you remember this bitch?"

"She…she…" The lump in his throat prevented the rest of the sentence from coming out.

"Lemme help. That's the bitch you were s'posed to take care of for me, ain't it?"

Bill pushed both hands over his brush cut and sat back. The temperature in the room had quickly climbed a few degrees. He squirmed uncomfortably in his seat.

"Nothin' to say?"

"That's her, Frank, but—"

"But what?"

"I *did* take care of her!"

"You did, huh?" Frank's glare intensified.

"I mean, I did what you told me to do."

Frank jerked a thumb at the screen. "*That* look like you took care of things?"

"Not really…"

"You're right about that. Know how I know? Cause she's standin' there beside a cab. Before that, she was talkin' to a damn cop. And right after that, she got back in the damn cab. Even the world's dumbest shithead knows you can't do *any* of those things when you're dead. She ain't dead, is she?"

"No, sir."

"Why isn't she dead, Billy boy?"

"I *thought* she was…"

"You *what*?"

92

"I thought she *was*."

"You're gonna have to explain that one to me."

"I wish I could."

Frank sat forward in his chair and picked up his glass. He finished what was in it, then put it back down. He was still glaring. "I'm gonna give you my undivided attention now, and you're gonna tell me why that bitch is still walkin' around, when just a couple weeks ago, I told you specifically to take care of her so she wouldn't be able to walk around ever again. Got it?"

Bill groaned.

"I *said*, got it?"

Bill nodded.

Frank shrugged. "Good. Now start talkin'. I want you to tell me why this bitch is still walkin' around when she should be fertilizin' the ground somewhere miles away from here."

DAY THREE

Chapter 9

Robert awoke the next morning and found that he was alone in the bed.

Somewhat disoriented, he sat up and listened.

Silence.

Where was Julie? Had something happened while he was asleep?

His thoughts automatically went back to the previous night, and he found himself grinning stupidly again, much like a child on Christmas morning gazing wide-eyed at the presents piled beneath the tree.

Once again he worried that the last three days had been a dream. A girl like Julie seemed entirely too good to be true. So did the circumstances leading up to what happened last night. A guy bumps into a beautiful babe, who turns out to be the most wonderful girl he's ever met in his life. And to top it all off, she also seems to feel the same about him.

Kind of far-fetched, isn't it?

But not impossible.

All right, then. If you think this is really happening, where the hell is she?

He had no idea. Since this was her place, he guessed she could be anywhere.

Then go look for her before you find out this really is a dream, and that you're actually lying in your own bed, imagining that you're waiting for the greatest woman you've ever seen to come back into the room and bang you half to death.

Once he realized he had just carried on a silly conversation with himself, he groaned and rubbed his eyes. This was ridiculous. The smart thing a reasonably intelligent man would do would be to find out what was going on.

Was he reasonably intelligent?

Or did he have all those people working for him brainwashed into imagining he was?

There was one way to find out, wasn't there?

He swung his legs over the side of the bed. Just as he was about to put on his clothes, the strong aroma of fresh coffee drifted into the room. Reality beckoned, and he smiled.

She was making coffee.

You idiot, you were all ready to cash it in. You thought she was an illusion. This was never real, was it? In your own little pessimistic world of failures and disappointments, a woman never *gets out of bed in the morning after a night of great sex and makes coffee, does she?*

He was being paranoid. And silly.

There was no other term for it. And, of course, no reason for it. Julie seemed to be just as taken by him as he was by her…so why would he think even for one moment that something should be wrong just because she wasn't lying beside him in the bed the moment he woke up?

The aroma of bacon and toast drifted into the room, and he suddenly realized just how hungry he was.

He hurriedly dressed, left the room, and hustled down the hall.

Julie was doing something at the kitchen counter. She had on fluffy pink slippers and a frilly light blue housecoat that came down to just below the knee. He didn't realize the housecoat was wide open until she caught him out of the corner of her eye, then turned and smiled. "I see you're finally up."

"The heavenly smells brought me close to a pleasant state of nirvana. So here I am." He tried his best not to stare, but he was a guy, after all. She hadn't put on her bra and wore only her black laced panties. He instantly discovered that he was much more awake than he'd been just moments earlier.

She noticed his dilemma and laughed. "I knew I should've tied this thing shut." She pulled two pieces of toast from the toaster, placed them on a small plate, picked up a butter knife, smeared butter over the toast, and brought the plate over to the table.

He met her just as she placed the plate on the table. "I'm *so* glad you decided against it." He wrapped his arms around her and they kissed.

She pulled away much too soon. After kissing him lightly on the cheek, she went back to the stove. "Sit and stay a while. I hope you're hungry."

"Famished." He poured coffee from the carafe and added sugar. "What do you normally do on Saturdays?"

"I usually go in to work. We're open on Saturdays, you know."

"All day?"

"It's our busiest day of the week."

"Then I guess I have to find other stuff to do today."

"I do have an assistant, you know…"

"Does that mean you're working today?"

"Not necessarily."

"Then you're *not* working today?"

"I didn't say that."

"What *are* you saying?"

"I'm saying I have an assistant. You *were* paying attention, weren't you?"

"I *think* I was…" He forced his attention away from the robe. "That thing's really doing a number on me…"

"Are you saying you're having a problem concentrating?"

"I'm saying that robe's really doing a number on me."

"I can close it, ya know…"

"Please don't."

"Only if you promise to pay attention."

"I promise."

"Good. Now…what were we talking about?"

"Keeping the robe open?"

"You're silly."

"We've already established that, haven't we? And I've learned to live with it."

"I think we were talking about whether or not I'm working today or leaving that to my assistant."

"You didn't say you were or you weren't. Which is it?"

"I didn't think we got that far."

"We didn't. I was distracted, remember?"

"Let's talk about that confusion thingy. Where exactly were we?"

"If you're going to work. If you aren't. If you're gonna spend the day with me. If you aren't. If your assistant's coming in. That sort of stuff."

"Would it bother you if I went in?"

"A little."

"Just a little?"

"You do have a business to run."

"How about if I go in for just a couple of hours?"

"Do you want me to go in with you?"

"Yes, but you don't have to."

"I'm confused again."

"I just don't want you to get bored."

"How about if I drive you to the shop and drop you off?"

"And then…?"

"I'll come back and pick you up when you call me."

"That sounds good." She brought over the eggs and put the plate in the center of the table. Before she sat, she kissed him full on the lips.

When the kiss ended, he said, "You really do need to close that robe."

"Is it really bothering you that much?"

"I'll let you figure that out."

She sighed and closed it, then tied it with the sash.

"Thank you."

"You're welcome. For now."

"When do you have to go in?"

She sat next to him and shrugged. "Whenever I want."

"In other words?"

"I'll leave that up to you."

"To do what?"

"To decide when I should consider getting dressed and going in."

"*Please* don't leave that up to me…"

***

After breakfast, they left the kitchen and were walking side by side down the hall when Julie suddenly stopped and stood very still.

He put his arm around her waist. "You okay?"

No response. She just stood there, staring straight ahead.

"Julie?"

Still nothing.

"What's wrong?" He gently squeezed her waist.

She smiled, but it wasn't one of her best efforts. "I'm…fine…"

He suddenly felt uneasy. The way she'd said it sounded like a lie. And her voice was strange. Weak and unsteady. He could tell she was hiding something from him.

"You sure?"

"You're not the only one who's smitten here, you know." She gave him another weak smile.

"You're saying *I* did that?"

She gave a loose shrug. "I don't see anyone else here—do you?"

He held her tightly to him as they went into the bedroom.

As she pulled away and moved rather awkwardly to the bathroom, he knew something wasn't quite right.

Chapter 10

Bill Torchia hadn't slept well at all.

As he shuffled into the bathroom and turned on the shower, he couldn't stop the horror from the previous evening from taking over his thoughts.

His spirits sank once again when he recalled sitting in Frank Baroni's office, looking up at the man while struggling to keep from crumbling. Convincing himself that he had to tell Frank exactly what happened and somehow make the big guy believe every word. This meant remembering every single detail that had transpired that evening just weeks earlier, when he'd first approached Julie Kenner.

He had to face the terrifying fact that he was toast. He could not possibly squirm out of this one, and the reason was simply that he couldn't tell his boss the most important detail of all.

He cursed himself once again for having turned this over to the Tripper. True, the little shit had a good rep and knew how to get things done. And when Bill gave him an extra five hundred for this special rush job, he was confident that the slimy dude would be especially diligent about this job.

But apparently he wasn't.

Julie Kenner was still walking around.

Once Frank had ordered Bill to tell him exactly what went wrong, Bill knew he had to set the record straight somehow, even though he had no idea how he could tell his story without sounding like a pathetic nutcase. But he had no choice. His boss would not put up with any bullshit. And since this matter hit Frank particularly close to home, the big guy would not tolerate *any* excuse, even if it made perfect sense.

The fear had taken over quickly. Bill couldn't contain it because of the anger oozing like molten lava from Frank Baroni's glaring eyes. Bill knew that he was a goner. But just then, something occurred to him that he hadn't thought of. It might have been the fear kicking in fresh adrenaline that triggered his brain to start working again. Whatever it was, it had pushed the fear to the side, giving him a sudden jolt of the sort of confidence he needed right then. And whatever this was that had kicked in convinced him that if he told his boss the truth, he just might be able to squeak out of this.

The Tripper was the one who should take the heat for this. Frank would be pissed at Bill for not doing the job himself, but he probably wouldn't make him bite the big one.

At least, he *hoped* he wouldn't.

Bill hated throwing anyone under the bus, but in this case, he had no choice. It was either him or the Tripper, and since the boss wanted to know what happened, Bill had to tell him.

"I didn't do the job myself, Boss." His heart pounded as he blurted it out. "I didn't think I could."

Frank's eyes narrowed. He appeared shocked by the revelation. Bill was relieved somehow because the anger appeared to have dimmed somewhat.

"What was the problem?"

102

Bill saw the anger coming back and struggled to keep it all together. He pointed to the laptop with a shaky hand. He truly hoped his boss would understand. There should be no reason why he shouldn't. Frank was a guy, too. And having the reputation for being a notorious womanizer, he appreciated gorgeous broads just like any other male with raging hormones. Frank was Italian, and no doubt owned a bunch of them. This made him the perfect candidate to sympathize. "Did you *see* that babe?"

"I saw her." Frank gave him a bored look. "So?"

Bill knew right then that he'd have to make his point even clearer. "Let me put it this way: if you saw her close up—"

"You're tellin' me you fucked up an important job 'cause you got a hard-on for this bitch?"

Bill shifted uncomfortably in the seat. This was going to be much more difficult than he'd hoped. "Sorry, but that's what happened, Boss…"

Frank was silent for nearly a minute as he stared at Bill with those deep-set dark eyes that had been known to turn grown men into quivering sacks of mush. He sat back and picked up one of his imported Italian cigars, which he would smoke on occasion when something was really bothering him. He picked it up, held it in front of his face, sniffed it, then regarded it silently for another minute or so, turning it around with his fingers, inspecting the tip, then studying the other end. After a while, still gazing at the cigar, he said, "You really expect me to believe that?"

"Like I said—"

"I heard you. I'm right here, just a couple feet away, listenin' to what sounds like total bullshit. You just said somethin' that makes no sense. None whatsoever. You been workin' for me how long now? Three years?"

"Closer to four."

"You never went against me before..."

"I didn't think I was, Boss."

"I told you to take care of her. You didn't do it. Whaddya call *that*?"

"Well, as I just told you, I didn't think I could do it myself, so I brought in someone who could."

"And who might that be?" Frank scowled and shook his head. "And don't tell me you hired that weasel, Tripper..."

Bill sighed tiredly and looked down at his lap.

"Goddammit!" Frank looked like he was about to have a heart attack. "That asshole's a worthless sack of shit!"

"He knows how to get things done, Boss..."

"He's a walkin' mental case. That idiot *likes* hurtin' people. He does it for kicks and would prob'ly do it for nothin'. He even *takes pictures* when he's finished. Prob'ly puts 'em in a scrapbook, for all we know. For a sick bastard like him, it could be just for shits and giggles."

"I just thought he could do the job—"

"Well, he obviously didn't, did he?"

"Apparently not."

Frank thought that over for a while. "All right, walk me through this."

"You mean, what the Tripper said? Or—"

"Forget that dirtbag. Tell me what happened that squeezed your balls so tight, you thought you had to squeak your ass outa this little venture by goin' behind my back."

"Boss, I didn't do it to go behind your—"

"Just start talkin'. Who knows? You might get lucky if I decide to be nice about this cluster fuck."

"Where should I start?"

"At the beginning, where the hell else? You followed this woman to her flower shop right off Semoran?"

"That's what I did…"

"What happened after that?"

"I found out that she owns the place and runs it with just one assistant, who looks like she's probably in her early twenties."

"What the hell does that have to do with—"

"I'm trying to give you every detail."

"All right, all right. Keep goin'…."

"She wasn't in the main area of the shop, and her assistant asked me what I wanted, so I asked where her boss was. She asked why I wanted to see her, and I said it was a personal matter."

"And then…?"

"She got out her cell, told her boss, and then she pointed where the office was and told me to go right on in."

"Keep goin'…"

Bill took a breath and rubbed his temples. This had been getting more difficult by the second. As his memory cleared, the image of that gorgeous woman standing behind her desk came right back, and so did his initial reaction. He would never forget that feeling. He knew the instant he got a good look at those big, beautiful blue eyes that there was no way he could do what Frank wanted him to do.

However, telling Frank about this feeling was going to be as impossible as anything he'd ever done in his life.

"I'm still waitin', Billy boy…"

Bill swallowed, then looked down at his lap. "I just…couldn't…do it, Boss."

"Why the hell not?"

"I don't know. Somethin' about her—"

"You wanted to fuck her."

"Yeah. No. It wasn't *that*. Not at *all*…"

"What the hell *was* it, then?"

"I *don't know*!" Bill got up and started pacing. "It was the way she was standing. The way she was looking at me."

"You felt *sorry* for this bitch?"

"It wasn't that, either!"

"You're not makin' sense, Billy boy."

"I know, I know. The only thing that made sense to me right then was that I couldn't do anything to a girl like her. Nothing! At all! And then I started thinking of how I could do something to her without actually looking her in the face." He shook his head and threw up his arms. "That thought didn't go anywhere, either!"

"I think I get it."

Bill stopped pacing. "You do?"

"I don't like it—not at all. But I get it. You couldn't do anything to this girl 'cause she got your engine runnin' and you knew you'd wimp out, so

106

you went to that Tripper psycho and paid *him* to do the deed. And by the way, sit your ass back down. You're makin' me dizzy, movin' around like that."

Bill dropped heavily into his chair. "I knew he could do it, boss. I knew he wouldn't wimp out."

"How'd ya know?"

"Tripper...well, as you said, he's wired different. He'd push his own mother down a flight of stairs for the right amount of money. He doesn't like anyone and has no friends. He likes it that way. I knew he'd be able to do something about this, so I just left the flower shop and got right on my cell."

"But that idiot didn't do it either, did he?"

Bill groaned. "No, sir..."

"Whaddya think happened?"

"I really don't know, Boss."

"Well, you know one thing, don'tcha?"

"What's that?"

"The girl's still walkin' around. Tripper fucked up, and because of it, she's still above ground. As long as she is, she can fry my ass for somethin' she saw. It's like this. I solved a problem that had been makin' life difficult for me and my old man, and ever since, things have been just fine. But life has this nasty habit of turnin' things around and tossin' old shit back in your face. If the wrong people suddenly get curious and decide to look into this, it might get the damn media morons stickin' their noses where they don't belong. And if this girl you've got the hots for gets wind of it, she just might decide to open her trap. If she does, my ass is gonna be entirely too damn close to a hot burner. Get it?"

Bill nodded.

"This means you gotta see this through, one way or the other."

"I know."

"First order of business? Find out what the hell happened with that Tripper psycho."

"Yes, Boss."

"Don't screw it up this time."

"I'll see to it first thing in the morning, Boss."

"See that you do."

Now, after a light breakfast of eggs and toast and several cups of strong black coffee, Bill left his apartment even angrier than he'd been when his boss showed him the video.

He didn't want to follow through with this in the first place. He was both glad and very relieved that Tripper hadn't done anything to the woman.

However, he knew where this left him.

His nerves twinged worse than ever as he slid behind the wheel of the Charger. He closed his eyes, sat back in the seat, and thought once again about those beautiful blue eyes. And although he realized that what he was thinking was totally unrealistic, he wanted so much to tell her that he honestly didn't want any of this to happen.

Julie Kenner, he thought miserably, *something really bad is gonna happen to you, and there's not a damned thing I can do about it...*

Just fifteen minutes later, his thoughts continued jumping wildly as he pulled onto the GreeneWay to make the short three-mile trip to the garage apartment off Primrose, where Tripper lived.

Chapter 11

Leonard Squalls was known by everyone as the "Tripper."

Leonard earned his nickname twenty years earlier, when he tripped a middle-aged man in a small crowd gathered at the corner of Church Street, sending him directly into the path of a tour bus that happened to be sailing by at that same moment.

The deadly "trip" was done perfectly, with the agility and skill of a professional dancer, without anyone within eyeshot suspicious enough to question the accident. And although Leonard was only eighteen at the time, that miniscule shift, in which he had turned his ankle a mere inch or so in the appropriate direction and used his elbow to tap the other man in the hip just enough to make him lose his balance, had taken Leonard just five seconds of his time, earning him a hundred bucks.

The money was given to him by a tall, well-dressed guy around forty who'd approached him fifteen minutes earlier, just as Leonard was about to enter a bar on that same block with a fake ID he'd bought from the high school bully for ten bucks. Like most others from that school, the bully hadn't liked Leonard at all and pushed him around at every given opportunity.

Leonard figured the big brute sold him the card just so he wouldn't be caught with it if he was pulled over by the cops for dealing meth. The bully earned more than five hundred bucks a week dealing meth and crack. This was an extremely worthwhile enterprise for an eleventh-grade flunky who lived by himself in someone's basement because his momma had left home months earlier with a skinny young black dude who considered himself to be the next messiah of hip hop.

The tall, well-dressed dude spotted Leonard outside the bar and gestured him over, where he stood at the corner, nervously smoking a cigarette and looking around as if expecting something bad to happen.

"Wanna make a hundred bucks, kid?"

Leonard noticed the gold watch on the man's skinny wrist as well as the pricey-looking pinky ring and three other rings that looked like they had cost this fancy dude some serious money. He also figured that whatever this dude wanted wasn't on the up and up. Leonard wasn't exactly a worldly individual but had enough sense to realize that anyone respectable wouldn't offer that much money to a kid he had never seen before.

But since Leonard had only eight bucks to his name and planned to use most of it on beer, he decided to at least listen to what the dude had to say.

The dude pointed to the corner of the next block. "In fifteen minutes, a man around fifty will be standing there, waiting for a bus. Think you can do something that might coax him out into the street?"

"You mean, like, in front of traffic?"

"That's exactly what I mean. Can ya do it?"

"I think so…" Leonard didn't care what had to be done. People had been treating him badly for

110

most of his young life, so he wasn't concerned much about what happened to any of them. He didn't even care what the guy in question had done to warrant this. He cared only about the money he was about to stuff into his pocket. "What's this dude look like?"

"He's about five-eight," the fancy guy said. "At least twenty, maybe even thirty pounds overweight."

"What color's his hair?"

"He's bald, with silvery gray stubble on the sides. He'll be wearing a light gray suit. Do it and the hundred's yours."

"Where will you be?"

"I won't be that close, but I'll be watching."

"When do I get paid?"

The man pulled his hand out of his jacket pocket. A single folded bill appeared between his thumb and forefinger. He handed it over. "Any problem?"

"No, sir!" Leonard gazed at the bill, then at the man. Something about all this felt really fishy. Leonard figured he could outrun this dude and make off with the money. But this seemed totally cool. Exciting, too. He'd never killed anyone before but had seen it done and figured it shouldn't be that hard. Anyway, he enjoyed looking at the bill and immediately began thinking about how he could spend the money.

"Then it's a deal?"

"You *trust* me?" Leonard asked, confused by the arrangement.

The man shrugged. "You look like you need the cash. Besides, you do this right, I'll probably need you again."

"For another hundred?"

A shrug. "Maybe even more."

"Seriously?"

The man nodded.

From that day on, Leonard had no trouble making money. He met the fancy dude four more times in the same area and earned more than three thousand bucks just by tripping, bumping, or nudging someone in the right direction at the right time. He learned how to do the job quickly and anonymously and was able to leave the scene long before anyone in the area even realized what had happened. The fact that Leonard was plain looking, never washed his hair or brushed his teeth, and dressed in sloppy old clothes, made things easy. No one noticed anything he was doing simply because no one liked looking at him or being close to him.

Over the years he'd made a great deal of money. He had come to the realization that just about everyone who had money always had an enemy they wanted out of the way. And it was painfully obvious that those with the most money always seemed to have the most enemies.

Frank Baroni, for example…

When Bill Torchia approached him just a few weeks ago, Leonard was standing at the end of a long line outside one of the lap dancing areas, where Luscious Sheila would be dancing that night. Luscious Sheila was the club's most popular dancer. It was known throughout Central Florida that Sheila

112

could not only drain any guy out of every cent he had walking into the place, but she could also have him waiting anxiously in line the very next night to drain him once again with another sizzling lap dance.

Though Leonard had been going to both Babes Aplenty and Club Venus nearly every weekend for the last five years, he had never been able to buy a lap dance with Luscious Sheila. That night, however, he intended to break his unlucky streak. He had wads of ready cash in his pockets and promised himself he wouldn't leave the club without being gratified by the legendary dancer.

But when Bill Torchia approached him and told him he wanted to talk to him outside the club, Leonard sensed trouble and decided it would be a smart—and healthy—move for him to change the evening's itinerary. To Leonard, this smelled strongly of Frank Baroni, so he didn't argue. He knew that the club's bouncers had been picked special by Baroni, and that you just didn't fuck with any of them. And if one of them approached you and told you he wanted you to walk outside with him, it most definitely involved Frank. Baroni's reputation as a dangerous badass with mob connections and a hair-trigger temper trumped everything else—including a chance with Luscious Sheila—and without hesitation he followed the tall, muscular, broad-shouldered dude down the hall leading to the EXIT sign.

"I got a job for you." Torchia seemed on edge as he stood a few feet from the EXIT door, out of sight of the overhead security camera. "It pays a grand, but I'll throw in an extra C-note if you do it quick."

"How quick?"

"An hour or less."

"When do ya want it done?"

"You're not gonna ask the details?"

Leonard knew better than ask questions. After twenty years of success, he didn't want to piss off the cash cow. The one common thing that always seemed to set people off was when you asked too many questions. "I figure you'll tell me what you think's important."

Bill reached into his pocket and pulled out a scrap of paper folded into a small square piece. "Address is on it."

Leonard took it, opened it, and looked at it. It was the address of a flower shop on Semoran. He looked up at Bill Torchia and frowned. "A *flower* shop?"

"The owner needs to be taken care of."

"He or she?"

"She."

"What's she look like?"

"You'll know her immediately. She's a brunette. Great body, long legs, big blue eyes."

"Okay..."

"Got any qualms about doing a babe?"

"Nope."

Torchia sighed and wiped his forehead with a big-knuckled hand. Tripper could tell the big dude was relieved. "By the way…it needs to be handled quietly."

"*All* mine are handled quietly."

"This one'll be no different, then."

"You got it."

***

Julie found herself in a serious dilemma.

After Robert parked the BMW behind the flower shop building and followed her inside, she struggled to concentrate on running the shop—not what happened less than an hour ago, in her condo.

However, as her focus continued to wane, she quickly found that she couldn't ignore the sensation. She realized that because of it, she was going to find it impossible to get on with her daily routine.

"You're *sure* you're okay?" Robert asked as they went down the hall that led to her office.

She knew it wouldn't take a genius to suspect something serious was going on. She'd felt his strong reaction back at the condo, when the sensation had first hit her. A glint of fear had shown in his eyes, and she knew right away that hiding anything from him was going to be difficult, if not impossible.

"Why do you ask?" She tried sounding casual.

"You don't *look* okay."

She decided to use a little distraction here. In this case, she would probably need to employ the usual feminine distraction arsenal. She didn't like deception, but this was serious, and she could think of no other way of handling it.

Sighing, she frowned and reached up to fluff her hair. "Is it my hair? I didn't think I should—"

"Your hair's perfect." His grim expression did not change.

115

"It must be the makeup, then. Since you were with me, I was kind of distracted, so I probably didn't—"

"The makeup's perfect. As usual, I can hardly tell you're wearing any."

"The skirt, maybe? I usually wear slacks for the Saturday crowd, but since you're with me, I decided to—"

"That skirt's dynamite." He still did not crack a smile. "I'm trying to ignore it right now because I'm struggling to keep my head focused."

"Focused?"

"On the real issue."

"The real *issue*?"

"You know what I'm talking about. And please stop repeating what I'm saying. It's making me even more suspicious."

So much for distraction…

But she still needed to make this as confusing for him as possible.

"Robert, you're not making this easy, you know…"

"I'm not trying to."

"In your own words, my hair is perfect. So is my makeup. And this skirt works for you as well. But I don't look okay. Please explain—"

"Whatever's going on with you has got nothing to do with your appearance."

This told her she was correct. He *did* know something serious had happened in the hall.

But she needed to know what he was thinking. The only thing she could glean from him right now was distrust, some anger, and a little fear.

"Robert, what exactly are we talking about?"

"When we left your kitchen, you suddenly stopped walking, and then the strangest expression took over your face."

She'd been right all along. "What sort of strange expression?"

"It was kind of hard to explain."

"Please try."

He paused for a few moments. "My first impression was that something frightened you."

"Really?" She needed to keep her emotions in check. Robert had just nailed it, but she couldn't possibly let him know how right he was. It would have been disastrous to tell him what really happened—that she had sensed a strong feeling telling her something bad was about to happen and that nothing could be done about it. "I looked that bad?"

"You didn't look bad at all."

"How *did* I look?"

"Frightened—as I said before."

She couldn't have him thinking he was right—even if he was. She had to handle this a certain way. Without scaring him off. "Really, Robert, I think you might be overreacting."

"To what?"

"In case you need to be reminded, I haven't been myself lately."

"Really? Who have you been?"

"Don't be cute, now." She could sense him softening already. "You know what I'm talking about."

"I give up. Why haven't you been yourself lately?"

She smiled and touched his cheek. "Look in the mirror, silly."

Chapter 12

The filthy black-and-white checkered Mini Cooper sitting in front of the garage apartment provided clear proof that Tripper was home.

Bill Torchia had brought along his .380 Beretta Tomcat but hoped there would be no need to use it. He didn't want to put Tripper in the ground and certainly didn't want to use it to scare the bastard. Guns tended to go off when you brought them out in plain view and aimed them at people. Some folks went into immediate shock and pissed their pants while others turned apeshit and forced you to use the gun if you wanted to stay alive. Still others tried toying with you until they thought your guard was down, then did something stupid.

Bill had only talked to Tripper a couple of times. He'd seen him at the club and had heard about him from various sources. Although Bill made his living tossing troublemakers out of the club, he didn't care much for people who made their living hurting or killing others. His ten-month stint in Iraq had opened his eyes to what people were capable of doing to one another. He'd learned entirely too much about inhumanity when he took part in the Battle of Haditha Dam and was given the unpleasant job of interrogating insurgent prisoners.

He hadn't wanted to hire Tripper in the first place. He did so because his only other option was to personally handle the job Frank Baroni had given him. Bill needed the job at the club. It was easy work and paid very well. However, Bill was no killer. He only roughed up people who deserved to be roughed up. He'd never roughed up a woman before and certainly never intended to do one in—ever.

Tripper was the most likely candidate to handle this because he always did things simply and had never shown evidence of a sadistic streak. He merely kicked, pushed, or tripped someone, forcing them into lethal danger, which caused instant death without suffering agonizing pain.

Short and simple. Then it was time to move on.

At the time, Bill had no idea why Frank would want such a classy woman dead. Knowing Frank as he did, as well as the company Frank kept and the business he conducted, he guessed that she had accidentally crossed paths with his boss and quite possibly had seen or heard something that would be disastrous for Frank if she ever confided in anyone about it.

Now that Frank had told him what had happened, Bill knew the whole story. His boss considered the woman a threat—case closed.

But even so, Bill could not personally handle such a loathsome act and chose to hand it over to someone else.

Despite much self-anger and embarrassment for passing the buck, Bill was confident that Tripper would act quickly, and that the woman wouldn't suffer.

Something had obviously gone wrong. The little runt hadn't delivered, and now Frank knew about it. And after years of dealing with the Baroni's, Bill was certain Carlo also knew.

Like it or not, Bill found himself trapped in the extremely precarious position of finding out exactly what the hell had happened.

Bill parked the Charger next to the Mini Cooper and carefully climbed the sixteen wobbly wooden steps leading to the one-bedroom apartment located above the two-stall garage. He knocked on the door and waited.

Nothing.

He was about to knock again when a muffled voice from inside said, "C'mon in."

Bill opened the door and groaned.

The area was a mess. Dirty laundry lay in scattered piles on the couch, armchair, and carpet. Filthy plates, dishes, and glasses cluttered the sink counter. A heavy mix of beer and B.O. assaulted his nostrils.

His long, scraggly brown hair filthy and unwashed, Tripper sat cross-legged in a corner of the messy couch. He was wearing a loose-fitting gray sweatshirt and matching gray sweatpants covered in stains. He gripped a bottle of Coors and held it in his lap. His eyes were glazed.

Great, Bill thought angrily. *This boy's shitfaced.*

"Hey there." He looked up at Bill and belched loudly. The little runt's bad breath reached Bill even though he was standing ten feet away. "Been expectin' ya."

This was just terrific. Bill knew right then that something terribly bad had happened. "We need to talk."

"C'mon in. Sorry the place is a mess, but what can I say?" Tripper belched once again and chuckled. "I never did get off doin' housework."

Annoyed and confused by the reception, Bill closed the door and hoped he wouldn't have to rough up the little guy.

And he certainly didn't want to use the .380 if things got messy.

**

After Robert left, Julie sat down at her desk and tried desperately to focus on the events of the day.

It didn't take her long to realize how difficult such a task would be. Ever since she was hit by that dark vibe back in her condo, nothing felt right. Everything seemed off-center and out of focus. She'd managed to shower, dress, and apply her makeup without totally messing up the works, but as she stood in front of the mirror, brushing her hair, she discovered that she couldn't keep her mind centered on the events of the day.

Even so, she couldn't exactly ignore what had happened. Nor could she explain it—not even to herself. Being slapped by a strange darkness had been unsettling. Dismissing its sharp, icy jab so she could enjoy Robert's warm, tender touch had proven nearly impossible.

Her fears had faded somewhat as Robert drove her to the shop. She was able to carry on a reasonably intelligent conversation with him along the way, but right now, just twenty minutes later, found that she couldn't remember what they were talking about. Their plans later in the day, perhaps? Something about what he needed to do when he went back to work on Monday? Or had he asked her a question or two about the flower shop?

As she obsessed over this, a hazy image blipped momentarily, and she suddenly remembered something that had happened several weeks earlier. It hadn't made much of an impression at the time, but for some peculiar reason she couldn't quite pin down, it had immediately slithered out of the darkness of her abandoned memories to become center stage in her consciousness.

The event took place the night she and her sister Janie had enjoyed a nice, pleasant dinner at Schiller's Steakhouse Supreme on East Colonial, where they liked to meet once or twice a month to enjoy each other's company and catch up on the latest gossip.

After she and Janie finished dinner, Julie told her sister to go on out to the car while she made a quick stop. Just a few minutes later, Julie left the ladies' room and made her way to the parking lot in the rear of the building, where Janie's white Nissan was parked. She pushed open the EXIT door, took two steps, and accidentally bumped into a tall, dark-haired, thickset man hurrying from the direction of the dumpster in the alley not far from the restaurant's kitchen.

Embarrassed by her awkwardness, she smiled and excused herself, but the man had been in too much of a hurry to say anything to her in return. Undaunted, Julie proceeded down the walk leading to the parking lot facing the restaurant.

She read something a day or so later about a murder in that same area. She didn't think too much about it at the time, but when a large, good-looking, broad-shouldered guy stepped into her office a few days later to gawk at her for a few seconds before turning away and abruptly leaving the shop, she sensed her suspicions growing wildly.

Then, to add to the confusion, a very strange little guy smelling strongly of B.O. came to the shop just a few days later to talk to her about a minor mishap outside the store the following week.

This was when she realized something significant had happened the night she bumped into that guy behind Schiller's.

"Lady," the little guy said as he approached her in the shop, "is that your gray Honda out there? Parked in front of this place?"

"Yes…"

She sensed a darkness emanating from him and suspected he wasn't being sincere. It made her wonder if this could have been some sort of scam.

"Sorry, but I think I just tapped your rear bumper with my rental."

"Were you parking behind me? Or did something else happen?"

"Well, I was pullin' into the space directly behind you when my foot slipped. I think I kinda tapped your bumper a little too hard on the side."

"Did you put a dent in it?"

A frown and a shrug. "Sorta…"

"It's all right. It probably won't amount to much. I'll just give you the phone number of my insurance company, and you can call your agent and have him—"

"I think maybe you oughta have a look at it first."

"That's all right. If it's just minor, I don't think it's necessary for me to—"

"I really think you oughta take a gander. Otherwise, I'll feel awfully guilty."

More darkness wafted over, and she knew right then that this was some sort of elaborate trick. He was entirely too determined to coax her outside. A quick assessment of the man's expression told her he was in a hurry and wanted to get this over with. It was at that very moment when the incident at the steakhouse with the big dark-haired guy flashed in her thoughts.

Someone didn't want you to see him, her inner voice whispered, sounding clearer than ever.

"All right, then." She led the way out through the front entrance and went down the street, where her car was parked. She inspected the rear bumper but saw nothing. This told her she was right about his intentions. But she had to play along. Even so, some inner sense told her not to get too close to him. "I don't see anything," she said. "Maybe you're exaggerating."

"It's on this side." He had already slipped between the two vehicles and was standing very close to the tan rental car as heavy traffic passed by, missing him by less than two feet.

He wants you to step out in traffic...

She was about to protest when the other voice, the one she'd been hearing occasionally ever since her beloved grandmother had passed, whispered in her ear.

125

Use your special gift, child...

This was when she fully realized that her grandmother would always be with her. The sweet old lady had not abandoned her at all.

And her special gift, as Gram had promised, would always protect her.

"I really don't think I want to do that," she said, concentrating on the little guy's face. He opened his mouth to say something, but she added very softly, "You wouldn't *want* me to do that, would you? You wouldn't *want* me to stand so close to all this traffic, would you?"

He opened his mouth once again, but she said, "Someone might hit me, and you really wouldn't want that to happen to me, would you?"

He abruptly closed his mouth. He shook himself, as if he'd just come out of a trance. A moment later, he glanced at his car, then at her. He shook himself again, moved closer to the car, opened the door, and got in.

Moments later, he pulled out of the space and joined the slow, steady flow.

Now, as she sat at her desk, her memory bringing all this back, she suddenly realized that the darkness that had sprung out at her earlier at the condo could be related to what had happened when she bumped into that big man behind the restaurant. She also knew that the man she'd bumped into was not a nice man. And that she might have been right when she guessed that he had done something very bad. It was probably something he didn't want anyone to know about. Something he suspected would get him into serious trouble.

126

Julie had inadvertently become a threat to him. Unless she was mistaken, he was terrified that she might mention his description to the wrong person if the topic came up.

She feared that she had not heard the last of that unpleasant situation. She also realized that she could not shake its grim conclusion.

Someone else was coming after her.

Someone very, very bad.

***

Bill Torchia didn't believe what the Tripper had just told him.

"You're saying that the job I gave you didn't set well with you. At all."

Tripper had another slug of Coors. He sighed heavily and shrugged. "Sometimes things just, well, fuck up."

Bill didn't care for that answer. For one thing, it didn't tell him anything. For another, it suggested the little bastard hadn't been up to the job. Tripper was leaving out details, and Bill was determined to find out what went wrong. "That doesn't quite cut it for me," he said sourly.

Tripper shrugged. "Didn't do much good for me, neither."

"What I'm saying is, I need a better picture."

"I don't know what else I can say."

"Humor me, okay? Just tell me in plain, simple language why you walked away from this job."

Another shrug. "I just couldn't do it."

Bill stayed just a few feet from the door, a respectable distance from the clutter. He didn't want to venture too far away from the outside world. It had nothing to do with fear; he just wanted to be as close to fresh air as possible. He'd suffered from claustrophobia in Iraq and realized that this dark, foul area wasn't much different from those caves he'd entered to clear out the insurgents. Those tunnels of darkness were laced with death, decay, and gunpowder. This area, though not nearly as confined, reeked of foulness and a despair he hadn't experienced in years.

Something had gone terribly wrong. Something that shouldn't have happened had apparently happened, and he wasn't sure what to do about it. All he knew was that he'd paid this little twerp good money to do a job for him and the job wasn't done. But instead of Tripper admitting what he'd done— rather *didn't* do—he was lounging on a filthy sofa in his soiled sweats, chugging down beer. To make things even more bizarre, he didn't appear the least bit frightened or nervous. This made Bill wonder if Tripper had completely lost his nut.

Or maybe he was high on something in addition to the beer.

But none of that mattered. The only thing Bill cared about was that Tripper had reneged on an important job, and in doing so, had tossed Bill under the bus. Bill had to find out exactly what happened before he reported back to Frank with the bad news.

"*Why* couldn't you do it?" he asked.

Tripper had another slug of beer. "Dunno." He shrugged a bony shoulder. "Just couldn't."

This was getting him nowhere.

128

"I paid you a shitload of money to do that job..."

"Right. I didn't. I fucked up. First time, too." Tripper shook his head.

"What am I supposed to do now? Just walk away and tell Frank you couldn't do it?"

Tripper pointed to the small, dusty end table shoved awkwardly against the far wall. A thick envelope lay on it beneath a large square glass ashtray. "There it is," Tripper said.

"There *what* is?"

"The money you gave me. It's all there. Every cent. Take it."

"You're serious?"

"Every cent ya gave me. It's in that envelope."

"You didn't spend *any* of it?"

"Nope."

"And you want me to take it back?"

"Yep."

"Just like that?"

"Just like that."

Bill stared at the little guy, expecting him to break out in laughter. He merely sat there with his beer, gazing off into space.

Yep, something was *way* the hell off. There was enough money in that envelope for this little shit to pay two months' rent. But he didn't want it. Not a penny of it.

"Let me get this straight. You don't *care* about the money?"

"Nope."

"Why not?"

A sigh. "Didn't earn it."

Weird, to say the least. Tripper didn't seem the conscientious type at all.

"I'm still trying to figure out why the hell you just walked off a job like that. You've never done that before, right?"

"Right."

"But you did it anyway."

"Yep."

"And you won't tell me why."

"Nope."

"Why not?"

"Because I don't *know*, dammit."

"You realize what's gonna happen when I tell Frank Baroni what you didn't do?"

Tripper nodded. "He's gonna prob'ly tell ya to take me for a ride out to one of the lakes."

"Don't you care?"

"*Course* I care!" Tripper sat bolt upright. "Whaddya think I am? Crazy?"

"But you won't do or say anything that might make this go even a little easier on you?"

"No can do."

"Why not?"

"'Cause it won't matter."

"What won't matter?"

"Whatever I say."

"Try me."

"Lemme ask *you* a question..."

Bill wasn't in the mood for games. "I didn't come here to answer you any—"

"Just do it, okay? Go with me on this. Just this once?"

"All right."

"That babe your boss wants dusted. Have ya seen 'er?"

Bill hoped this wasn't going where he didn't want it to go. "I saw her."

"In person?"

"In person."

"Up close?"

Bill swallowed a lump in his throat. "How close?"

"Close enough to see those eyes."

Bill opened his mouth to reply, but Tripper was faster.

"They're blue. *Deep* blue. And *big*. *Real* big. And they're kinda, like, weird. Almost…magical. Know what I mean?"

"I've seen her eyes…" Bill thought it best to stay objective.

"There's somethin' about 'em, ya know."

Bill felt a sudden twinge in his lower spine. This was getting much too unreal. "What are you talking about now?"

"When ya first saw 'em… Tell me they didn't pull ya in."

"Howzat?"

"Tell me this chick's eyes didn't do a number on ya."

"Tripper, I think I know what you're trying to say—"

"Ever hold a fresh little puppy in your hands?"

"*What*?" Bill began wondering if this boy actually *was* going off the deep end.

"A puppy. A teeny tiny dog, right outa the mother—"

"I know what a newborn puppy is."

"Ever hold one?"

"I've had several dogs in my life."

"Ever hold one in your hands and think, If anyone ever hurts this little guy, if anyone ever looks cross-eyed at 'im, I'm gonna fuckin' kill the son of a bitch?"

Bill didn't reply. He knew exactly what Tripper was talking about.

Puddles, the tiny beagle puppy Bill's older brother brought home one day from high school, immediately came to mind. The little guy had been dropped off and was wandering around dangerously close to the road when Bobbie spotted it on his way home from football practice.

Jack gave the little guy to Bill, who held him lovingly in his arms, knowing the puppy belonged to him. And all he kept thinking was that no one would ever hurt the little guy ever again.

There I was, nine years old, holding an abandoned puppy in my arms, all eighty-seven pounds of me ready to kill anyone who ever got too close to that little guy…

Tripper was grinning at him. "Ya know what I'm talkin' about, don'tcha?"

Bill didn't reply.

"I know ya do…so don't try'n con me."

Bill remembered the day Puddles died just three short years later. The little guy died and left a giant hole in his heart. A hole he could still feel, even after nearly thirty years.

"To make things simple, lemme say this… I felt the same way when that babe flashed those baby blues at me."

Bill knew exactly what Tripper was talking about. However, none of this was relevant. He had to tell Frank *some*thing but knew that it couldn't possibly be what they were talking about right now. Telling his boss neither Bill nor Tripper could do any harm to the brunette babe because of her gorgeous, hypnotic blue eyes would not go over well at all.

"In other words," he said flatly, "you're saying there is no way in hell you're going to go back there and do what you didn't do before, when you had the chance."

Tripper sat up abruptly. His glazed eyes suddenly seemed very clear. But this time, a spark of fear flared in them as well. "Want an explanation? Here it is. It don't matter when or how Frank Baroni lights me up, there's no way in hell I'm ever gonna hurt that woman."

Chapter 13

At 2:00, Julie finally realized that she could not concentrate on her work at the shop.

She told Gwen that she could close up at three. Although she felt guilty for leaving early, she knew full well that she'd make a shambles of things if she stayed and tried conducting business. It had become painfully clear that she couldn't stay focused on anything. She found her mind wandering each time she was approached by a customer and asked simple questions. She also found that she could not remember certain details about some of her products, which made her feel totally incompetent. The last straw was when she was asked by a concerned customer if she wasn't feeling well and needed to lie down.

Before depression could sweep in and take full control, she called Robert and asked him to pick her up.

"Where would you like to go after I get there?" he asked.

"My condo." She wasn't in the mood to spend the rest of the afternoon fighting crowds at the mall or struggling to enjoy dinner in a fancy restaurant. Not with what was weighing so heavily on her mind.

"Hmmm…"

"What's that for?"

"I was thinking more along the lines of another dining experience. You know, I suggest a place and you say, "No, baby, I'd rather go here," or "Yes, baby, that sounds like a terrific idea.'"" When she didn't respond right off, he said, "I admit I might have stretched things a little with the "baby" bit, but—"

"You didn't."

"You're sure?"

"I'm sure. Baby."

"That sounded terrific. But getting back to our discussion... Are you positive?"

"Yes." She could tell he'd picked up something in her tone. "Why?"

"I don't know. I guess I didn't like the silence on your end when I finished my pretend scenario. It made me think that you might have something else in mind."

She knew she should have been more agreeable, but she just couldn't stop obsessing over what had happened that morning.

"I'm sorry," she told him. "I've got a lot on my mind lately."

"Me, too. Wanna know what's been on my mind? Or should I just make things simple and say your name right off?"

In spite of her dark mood, she laughed. As usual, Robert had instantly provided the perfect distraction. "Back atcha. But I'm sure you know that by now."

"That's why I've been thinking about you ever since I dropped you off. Give me fifteen minutes and I'll be right there, ready to sweep you away again."

His statement proved to be just what she wanted to hear. She suspected that he was quite aware that she'd been thinking about him all day, too. However, he couldn't possibly know what else she'd been thinking about. What had happened six weeks earlier was something she really hadn't thought too much of at the time. It bothered her at first, of course, but she kept telling herself that all she'd done was bump into someone. The same thing happened all the time to just about everyone, so why obsess over it?

But what had happened just days after, though weird and somewhat frightening, should have put her antennae on red alert. A guy coming into her shop, then turning around and running out of the shop after one glimpse of her? Then, only a day later, a strange little man showing up, insisting that she should follow him outside to look at the damage he had done to her car?

She knew she should have been satisfied that everything had worked out. She'd handled things the way she'd handled other situations. And in doing so, hoped she wouldn't hear anything about it again.

Unfortunately, this didn't happen.

She should have known something strange might result from that near fatal collision two days earlier, with all those cell phones waving about, pointed at the wreckage, the crowd, and everything else. But since she'd been so flustered by the accident and worried about Robert's perception of the event, she hadn't given anything else much thought.

But now she realized how foolish she'd been. Bad things had indeed happened. But instead of them ending, it appeared that the results were quickly coming back. Someone had seen her on YouTube, and because of it, the restaurant incident had come back to haunt her.

But this time, things would be even worse.

Like it or not, Robert was involved, and she was going to have to tell him about it.

She also feared that he would have to know every single detail about her.

***

Overwhelmed by fear and frustration, Bill Torchia trudged down the carpeted hall leading to Frank Baroni's office.

He knew damned well that what he had to tell his boss would not go over well. Worse, he didn't think Frank would even believe him.

Bill couldn't blame his boss one bit. After all, if he hadn't personally seen and talked to the woman, he wouldn't even believe such a story.

But it was true. Every word Tripper had told him was right on. Everything the little guy had said about this woman brought back a ton of emotion Bill hadn't felt in quite a while.

He had known a lot of women, and while just about every one of them possessed the same sort of power over men that develops naturally when a young girl becomes a woman, Bill had never known anyone else who had been so capable of totally mesmerizing a man.

The woman Tripper was talking about, that same woman Bill had seen just once, seemed to possess superhuman powers he had never personally experienced before. He couldn't possibly know if she was consciously aware of what she was doing, or intentionally used this extraordinary talent to achieve whatever goal or solve any problem she faced. Bill had never believed any woman could capture his heart so quickly. This girl Julie Kenner had done it, and each time he thought of those beautiful blue eyes, he felt himself melting all over again.

But that was beside the point. This woman posed a threat to Frank Baroni, and Bill had to come to terms with the cold fact that something had to be done to permanently eliminate this threat.

Tripper would also have to be dealt with, but on a different level. Since his usefulness would be taken into consideration, hc would not be looking at a death sentence. He would, however, face considerable accountability for not fulfilling a contract. This sort of behavior would not fare well in the arena he had chosen for his rare, sought-after skills. Because of his negligence, several extremely important, highly connected people were going to demand some form of retribution.

This starts with me, Bill told himself as he plodded uneasily down the long, carpeted hall. *I fucked up, and because of it, a slew of well-connected people are gonna be extremely reluctant to do business with Frank again. They're probably gonna be so nervous about all this that they'll quite possibly pay someone a handsome amount of money to make sure I don't rock the boat.*

Could he talk his way out of this one?

As he thought it over, he realized that the only way out of this was probably the most logical. This meant that his punishment would no doubt be what Frank had ordered him to do in the first place.

He would be forced to eliminate the woman himself this time. There could be no two ways about it.

I'm toast, he kept telling himself as he neared the office door in the same vein as a prisoner approaching the awaiting guillotine. *I either kill this beautiful girl, or I just turn the gun on myself. There's no other way.*

And with these dark, terrifying thoughts filling his head, he cautiously approached the door marked *Frank Baroni, Executive Manager*, and stood totally still, staring numbly at the nameplate. Then, after two solid minutes of wishing to disappear and realizing that he did not have the power to do so, he knocked nervously on the door.

Chapter 14

"Please tell me what's wrong, Julie…"

Robert didn't look at her as he drove the BMW. Slouched in his seat, he drove tensely, his eyes fixed on the busy highway straight ahead.

She could tell he was struggling with what had been happening with her. And why shouldn't he be suspicious? She'd been sending out all sorts of signals ever since that scary little episode this morning. She could only imagine how she looked. Judging by how hard that dark cloud had hit her, she guessed that she had the look of someone who had just been scared half to death.

Robert could tell something was very wrong. He'd asked her right off, hadn't he? And he'd touched her right after she'd stumbled. He'd no doubt felt her trembling, the coldness of her skin.

"It has something to do with what happened this morning after breakfast, doesn't it?" he asked after the heavy silence.

It took her several moments to realize that she hadn't answered his first question.

She couldn't possibly lie to him. Even if she wanted to, there was no reason for it. Like it or not, she needed his help. "Yes."

He waited for more of an explanation. When she didn't say anything, he said, "Does this have anything to do with…me?"

"Of course not." She couldn't believe he was worried about that. It was at that moment that she fully realized just how much damage her silence was doing to their growing relationship.

"You're sure?"

"Absolutely." She placed her hand firmly on his thigh.

He put his own hand on top of hers, which reassured her. "I just want you to know that if it does, you can talk to me, and I promise I'll try to—"

"We do need to talk, Robert..."

"Oh boy..." He sighed heavily, and his hand slipped on the wheel. The BMW swerved, lightly tapping the curb. "If I did something—"

"As I just said, this has nothing to do with you."

"But you also said—"

"We really do need to talk."

"About what?"

"This is about...me."

He went silent once again and stayed this way, watching the road ahead as he drove. When he spoke again, his voice had grown softer, nervous. Unsteady. "Does this...have anything to do with...what happened on Semoran? The accident?"

He'd figured it out. It was good in a way, but also bad, because she knew right then that their "talk" had already begun. And she had no other direction to go from here but forward.

"Yes."

"Your sixth sense?"

"It's more than just a sixth sense, Robert."

He glanced at her, then turned back to face the windshield. "You're not gonna tell me you can see the future, are you?"

"Not exactly…"

"Does that mean you *can't* see the future? Or does it mean that you're not gonna tell me?"

"It's not that at all."

"Then what *are* you talking about?"

She sighed deeply and felt herself tensing up. *Let it out. He has to know, and there's only one way for that to happen.*

Tell him, child…he deserves to know…

The voice was exactly what she needed just then to give her the boost she'd been searching for. "There are people…coming after me."

He stiffened in his seat. The BMW bumped the curb once again. "*What*?"

"People are coming after me."

He glanced in the rearview, then the side mirror. "What *kind* of people?"

"Bad people."

"Are you sure?"

She nodded.

"They're actually coming after you?"

"Yes."

"Why?"

"I'm pretty sure they want me dead."

***

Frank Baroni sat behind his desk, sipping Scotch while glaring at Bill Torchia.

Frank couldn't help feeling total disgust for the bastard. He wanted to haul off and slap some sense into the oversized idiot. Torchia was smart as well as a decent, stand-up employee, but for some reason Frank just could not understand, the bastard lacked the balls needed for certain jobs. Which was why

142

Frank would probably be forced to give him his walking papers.

When you demanded loyalty from someone who'd just turned tail on you, it was time to shitcan the relationship.

Take care of her. The message was simple. Find the woman, take her somewhere, put out her lights, then dump her. No fuss, no muss. No explanations were necessary. She wasn't important. Hell, she probably wouldn't even be missed. She was just some meddlesome bitch and could make things bad for Frank. In other words, she needed to be taken out of the picture. Permanently.

So then, what do you do? You handle it—what else? You don't delegate the work to a crazy little psycho who pushes people into traffic, you suck it up, use the balls you've been carrying around all your life, and do the damned thing yourself.

But no. Torchia turned wimp and let the crazy little psycho out of his cage.

And now he would have to pay dearly.

Torchia looked like he was trying to hide behind the chair. Six-three, two-twenty, all of it hard muscle, and could probably bench four hundred pounds...and this fool was trying to hide behind a fucking *chair*. Where the hell had all the men with the serious 'nads gone nowadays? Frank wanted to puke when he thought of what society had turned dudes into.

"I take it you saw the little runt?" he asked.

Torchia nodded.

"Then I guess you two discussed what happened, yes?"

"Y-yes, sir…"

"All right, then. Tell me what happened."

"Tripper said he couldn't do the job."

Couldn't do the job. What the hell did *that* mean? Torchia pays an idiot good money to take out a bitch, and six weeks later, this same bitch is seen in YouTube, walking around an accident scene, talking to a damn *cop,* for God's sake!

"Lemme get this clear. He couldn't do the job?"

"That's what he said."

"Did you ask him why?"

"He said he couldn't do it."

Frank finished his Scotch and poured more from the bottle. This wasn't making any sense. "Is there somethin' I'm not gettin' here?"

"It was a…a *personal* thing, boss." Torchia continued avoiding Frank's eyes.

"Personal?"

A nod.

"Define personal."

"Well, in short, he said there was no way he was gonna do anything in this world to hurt the girl."

Frank waited for him to say more, but Torchia had obviously finished his explanation. "That was it?"

Torchia nodded.

"You paid this asshole what? A coupla k for this?"

"Just about."

"And this was all you got?"

"He gave it back."

"Huh?"

144

"He gave me back the money."

"He *what*?"

"It was lying in an envelope in his place. The same envelope I used to give to him. He told me to take it."

Frank couldn't digest any of this. A hitter returning money for a soured hit? This sounded like something that should be listed in the Guinness Book of World Records. "He *told* you to take it."

A nod.

"A small-time hitter gave you back your money for a hit he couldn't do."

Another nod.

"Doesn't this seem kinda, well, odd?"

Torchia shrugged.

This made no sense at all. Frank had known and dealt with several hitters in his time. The very few who had botched up a job either skipped town *with* the money or ate their own gun.

"I don't think I've ever come across somethin' that weird before."

Torchia didn't reply.

"So then, he gave you back all that money because he told you there was no way he would do anything to the woman you paid him to hit?"

Torchia sighed and stared at the floor.

Frank was getting tired of all this. Bad enough the job didn't go as planned. But Torchia was acting like a pathetic wimp, and Frank didn't want wimps working in his place. "Is the damned *floor* tellin' you anything?"

Torchia looked up. "Boss?"

"I asked you a question and you answered me by keepin' your yap shut and starin' at the floor. I just asked if it cleared up anything."

"Boss, Tripper couldn't do anything because I kind of suspect the girl did a number on him."

"A number?"

Torchia nodded.

"You're gonna have to explain that one."

"She's got these big blue eyes—"

Dammit, here we go again…

"We've been through this before. You told me why you gave the job to Tripper. You said it was because this female got your engine runnin', and you knew you'd wimp out and blow the job. So now here we are, talkin' about a babe with big blue eyes. Is *this* why you get all worked up when ya think of this female?"

"Well, all I can say is that when you look at them, they do this number on you."

"Big blue eyes. Yeah. Whatever. And they do a *number* on you."

"Yes, sir."

"What sorta number?"

"You kinda, well, you want to protect her. She seems so…good. And nice. She makes you feel good inside." Torchia shook his head and frowned. "I really can't explain it any better than that, Boss."

Frank studied Torchia's face for a few moments before he spoke again. "Ya know ya work in a strip club, right?"

"Yes, sir..."

"And I guess you've also noticed that there are quite a few babes workin' here as well."

146

Torchia nodded.

"This female we're talkin' about... She's the first babe you've ever seen with big blue eyes?"

"No sir, but—"

"But what?"

"It's kinda like I just said, Boss..."

Frank could tell by Torchia's reaction this woman had obviously done the same number on him that she'd done on that nutjob Tripper. "This same shit goes for the runt, too, I take it?"

"Y-Yes, sir."

"She did a number on both of you?"

Torchia nodded.

"What sorta number are we talkin' about here? That protection/feel-good thing?"

"Boss, I know it sounds weird, but—"

"It sounds worse than weird. It sounds like you might need a padded room, a straitjacket, and a daily regimen of strong meds."

"It's true. I don't know how she does it, but when she looks at you, you want to make sure she's okay, and that nothing will ever harm her again."

"You're an idiot."

Torchia sighed tiredly, then nodded.

"You agree?"

"I don't know if I'm an idiot, sir, but I do know one thing."

"What's that?"

"I could never do anything to hurt that girl, either."

Frank finished his Scotch, sat back in his chair, and studied the other man. This sounded just as weird as anything he'd ever heard before. But no matter what had happened to Tripper and Torchia, this situation did not change. The woman had been in the wrong place at the wrong time. She'd seen something she shouldn't have, and she had to be taken out.

"Guess what?" Frank sat forward and looked Torchia square in the eye. "I've got a brand-new proposal for you, and you're either gonna accept it or I'm gonna have to re-evaluate your future with the club."

Torchia didn't reply.

"The situation is very simple. This girl can cause me a shitload of trouble, *capisc*?"

A nod.

"You know what I think of trouble, don'tcha?"

Another nod.

"Tell me what *you* think *I* think of trouble."

Torchia sighed. "You hate it."

"That's right. So nice that we're finally on the same page. Now…here's my proposal. You either handle this by yourself, or you come in here and tell me you can't handle it at all, and *I'll* handle it by bringin' someone else in to do it. I don't really want to because I don't want to bring anyone else into this, for obvious reasons. The less people who know about this, the better. But if I have to bring in someone else, you can bet your pathetic ass that this guy'll get the job done and he'll get it done fast. Get it?"

Torchia didn't reply.

"You heard what I said. You can't do it yourself? Tell me, and I'll make my own arrangements."

148

"You mean—"

"You know damn well what I mean. And you know damn well what this'll mean for your career."

"I still don't know if I'll be able to do this—"

"If you can't do it by yourself, I'll find someone to help you. I've got eight bouncers workin' this club, and you know every damn one of 'em. I know damn well that I can find one or two to help you take care of one meddlesome female. *Capisc?*"

A nod.

"Good. One thing you oughta know: if you end up wimpin' out on me again, I'm gonna be so fuckin' pissed, you'll wish you were never born. I'll make it so you'll never work in this town—or this *state*—again. Got it?"

"Yes, sir."

"That would be reckless as well as stupid. Do I seem the reckless or stupid type to you, Billy boy?"

"No, sir."

"All right, then. Now go find her and finish the damn job."

Torchia let go of the chair, turned, and began walking to the office door.

"One other thing."

Torchia stopped abruptly and turned around.

"If those big blue eyes of hers bother you so damn much, just do somethin' about 'em."

"S-Sir?"

"There's a remedy for a problem like that, ya know."

"A…remedy?"

"It's called a blindfold. It can be a scarf, a hankie, a pillowcase—even a coupla yards of duct tape. Just slip whatever the hell you've got right over those big blue eyes and guess what? It solves the problem and makes everything much easier. And if she squawks about it, wrap a few yards of that sticky stuff over those lips. That'll keep down the noise till it's time to put out her lights. Get where I'm comin' from *now*?"

Chapter 15

"People actually want you dead?"

Robert had stopped moving once he'd reached the kitchen doorway. He stared oddly at Julie as she opened the cabinet door and grabbed a small bottle of Kentucky bourbon.

His expression frightened her. He was pale, and she could clearly see the anxiety in his eyes. She also sensed the cold fear emanating heavily from him and wanted to scold herself for causing this. But it had been necessary. If he truly wanted a relationship with her, this was bound to come up again—and very soon. And what would she tell him when he asked her about it? She couldn't shrug it off. Or, even worse, lie to him and hope for the best.

He had to know, and she was determined to tell him.

"Yes."

"You're sure?"

"Not absolutely, but I wouldn't bet against it."

Robert thought that over. Then, sighing deeply, he walked over to the kitchen table and sat. Julie sensed that he was trying to get a grip on all this before saying anything else.

She hoped this wouldn't jinx anything. Right now, their relationship mattered more to her than anything else. Having dangerous men looking for her was bad, but she was confident that she could handle whatever fate tossed at her. However, she had no idea how she could possibly endure any of this if Robert decided he didn't want to be part of it.

She watched him and waited. And prayed he wouldn't be scared off.

You'll be okay, her inner voice whispered.

I hope so, she thought, her heart on the verge of breaking. *I really and truly hope so.*

Have faith, child...

I'll try...

"Don't you think you need to tell me what's really going on? I'm kind of in the dark here," Robert finally said.

"I know, and I'm sorry. I just—"

"You just what?"

She didn't want him to know her fears. Her heart pounded heavily as she struggled for a suitable explanation.

"Let me take a wild guess." He was watching her closely. "You were afraid something like this would scare me off?"

She couldn't reply; she just nodded.

"Really?"

She gave another nod.

"Well?" He shrugged. "Does it look like I'm gonna jump up and run out of here, screaming like a lunatic?"

It was at that moment that she wanted to wrap her arms around him and hold on to him forever. But before she could even begin to feel relieved, he said, "Tell me about it. I mean everything. And don't leave anything out, okay?"

"Where would you like me to start?"

A shrug. "At the beginning—where else?"

Her thoughts immediately went berserk. She suddenly discovered that she couldn't decide where exactly where this started.

"Tell me about these people who want you dead," he said softly.

It was right then that she knew where her story began.

She told him about the incident at Schiller's Restaurant, where she bumped into the large, mean-eyed man. From there, she continued with the big, good-looking guy coming into the shop just a few days later. She ended her tale with the smelly little guy who came into the shop right after that and tried to coax her into walking out into traffic.

Robert sat in total silence, his eyes glued to her as he listened to every word. She could tell he was paying attention. She could also tell by the way he sat that he wasn't going anywhere. This told her that he believed her and would not leave.

Once again, she wanted to wrap her arms around him and cling to him.

"Then you think those two guys who came to the shop were part of all this?" he finally asked.

"I'd bet on it."

"You're certain?"

"I can't think of any other reason something like that would happen." She picked up two glasses and brought them and the bourbon bottle over to the table. Even though she knew by this time that things might just be okay, she still found that she was waiting for him to suddenly get up and walk out of the room.

Robert took the bourbon bottle and poured two inches into each glass. "If I were in your situation, I'd probably be thinking the same thing."

She sat down facing him. "As I've said, I can't think of anything else that would make any of this happen."

Robert sipped the bourbon and stared at her. She could tell he was troubled by all this. She couldn't blame him because she was bummed out about it as well.

This whole situation was frightening. Julie was convinced that if it hadn't been for her gift, the incident at the store would have turned out very badly. She would not have been able to sense the little guy's intentions and, as a result, would have stepped out into the street and been killed.

"Walk me through what happened, step by step, when you went outside with him," Robert said.

"I went over to my car and looked at it."

"How much damage did he do?"

"There *was* no damage."

"None? At all?"

She shook her head. "His rental car was parked about two feet behind the Nissan, sitting at least a foot from the curve. But when I told him I didn't see any damage, that was when he circled his car and told me to check out the other side. He said the left side was where he'd bumped into me and that there was a little dent right there, on the other side of the bumper."

Robert's forehead wrinkled. "He would have had to be moving *past* your car, then swerve into the side panel, to cause the damage he was talking about."

"He didn't."

"Then you were right. He wanted you to step out into the street."

"Apparently…"

"Was there any traffic?"

"It was late into the lunch hour, so yes, there was a great deal of traffic."

"And if you did manage to step out into the middle of the street, you would have probably been hit."

"I'm one hundred percent certain."

"But you obviously didn't."

"I strongly suspected that the moment I did, he was going to rush over and nudge or bump me, which would have caused me to stumble into traffic."

"You're absolutely sure about that?"

Julie regarded the bourbon in her glass. She really hadn't wanted to tell Robert everything all at once, but the circumstances had quickly changed. He really had to know everything there was about all this. But when she saw the concern in his eyes, she realized that telling him everything would be the right thing to do. Because of her growing feelings for him, she would have to share much more of herself than she had ever shared with anyone. And she somehow suspected that her grandmother would agree.

"Absolutely," she said.

"No doubts whatsoever?"

"None."

He didn't reply. She could tell by his rapidly growing confusion that he was having trouble trying to piece this all together.

This was the moment she'd been dreading.

Tell him, child...he'll understand...

"I...have this gift," she said in a soft voice.

"Your sixth sense?" Robert shrugged. "You told me this before. It happened when you screamed at the cabby to stop before we –"

"That's not what it is, actually..."

"What *is* it, then?"

"It's...kind of hard to explain."

"Okay..."

She didn't know what to say. She was still worried that this might be too much for him and that he might not want to be involved.

Or worse—he might not believe her.

But he had to know, didn't he?

Of course he did.

Trust him...

Robert took another sip, put the glass down, and sat back. She sensed understanding and sympathy and found once again that she wanted to wrap her arms around him. "Well, I'm not going anywhere, so I guess you can take all the time you need. Just do me a large favor and explain it so I might actually understand what's going on."

***

Bill Torchia had one of two choices, neither of which appealed to him.

He either snuffed out the life of a beautiful young woman all by himself or joined forces with one or two of his cronies and planned the

156

kidnapping of this woman, which would result in her senseless murder.

You're no killer, he kept reminding himself over and over as he made his rounds down the hall at the club, which led to the lap dancing areas.

Funny thing, though. He'd reminded himself of this very same thing during his stint in Iraq, when he was forced to interrogate captured insurgents found among the rubble of bombed structures.

He had always made a special effort never to go back there and relive those horrible, blood-filled days. Most of the time, he was fortunate to block much of it from his mind. Many sessions spent with the Army psychologists prior to his discharge had helped. There had been entirely too many sleepless nights, too many times spent forcing himself awake to escape the nightmares of blood-filled images of torture and horrible, agonizing death. As a result of his therapy, he had eventually reached a point where he managed to control nearly 80% of his thoughts. Even so, there were times when he was not able to concentrate. When those intermittent occasions presented themselves, vodka came to the rescue, dimming the most potent of nightmares.

In this case, vodka could not possibly serve as a suitable remedy. How in God's name could he conceivably justify the cold-blooded murder of an innocent young woman? How could he live with himself? How could he make it through the night without the benefit of booze or heavy-duty meds? How could he ever look at himself in the mirror again?

He had no choice. Since he knew full well that he couldn't possibly do something so despicable, he'd have to leave Orlando. He would have to find somewhere else to live as quickly as possible. Somewhere far from this place. He couldn't work for a man like Frank Baroni, who obviously had no regard for human life. And he couldn't in clear conscience obey an insane order that would force him to change his life forever.

Worse, he couldn't possibly tell his boss that he refused the order—especially after Frank had given him just enough details that could be used against the big man in a court of law.

His head filled with dark thoughts and frightening images, he lumbered down the hall that led to the front room, where the main bar was located. Along the way he passed small groups of businessmen, every one of them slightly drunk and excited at the prospect of paying for a lap dance with one of the many gorgeous dancers in the club. He saw no trouble here, which meant that he had to return to the main room and keep an eye on the customers at the bar, who often showed disrespect to the waitresses by groping or rubbing against them at every given opportunity.

He needed to think. And come up with something that would work. Something that would somehow get him out of this complicated scenario. Otherwise, Frank would get suspicious and send someone looking for him.

Just as he went down the three carpeted steps that led to the east end of the forty-foot-long, L-shaped bar, Jocko Baines, the big, broad-shouldered

158

brute from Miami, motioned him over to where he was leaning against the counter.

Somewhat wary, Bill approached him.

Jocko gave him a sly wink. "Hear the Boss wants ya to do a special job."

Bill sighed tiredly. *Great. If this ape knows about it, Frank already arranged for this.*

"Told me to tag along." Jocko looked interested. "'Kay with you?"

Bill didn't like this one bit but had no idea how to deal with it. Once Frank had enlisted someone else, the whole thing was bound to turn out badly. "Listen, Jocko—"

"He said ya might need some coaxin'." The big man chuckled. "Sound about right?"

Bill remained staring and didn't comment.

Jocko pulled a cigarette out from his shirt pocket and stuck it in a corner of his mouth. "Gotta have a smoke."

"Who's covering the room?"

"Aaron's got it. Should be comin' outa the shitter in a few. Let's talk outside."

Bill's heart hammered as he followed the big brute out through the heavy rear EXIT door.

***

"Frank says there should be a bill or two in it for me."

Jocko Baines pulled in cigarette smoke and pushed it back out into the warm evening air.

Bill said nothing as the heavy stream of Orange Blossom traffic roared by. He was steamed at Frank for bringing in Baines and wondered how the hell

159

he could handle this without it turning into a blazing shit storm.

He knew right off how hopeless this was. Frank wanted the girl taken out, short and simple. Frank was furious about the Tripper fiasco and knew he could no longer trust Bill, so Baines was brought in for insurance. It was widely known that Frank preferred using thugs for dirty jobs. He'd chosen Jocko before, when dealing with snitches. And in another case, a drug trafficker. And everyone knew Jocko Baines was sadistic and didn't care much about anyone's feelings.

This was just about as hopeless as a situation could get.

"What's he payin' ya?" Jocko asked.

Bill knew that his best bet was to find out everything Frank had told Jocko about this. He didn't want to say too much. The less he told Baines, the more control he had of the situation.

Having *some* control was better than having none at all.

"What exactly did Frank tell you about this?" he asked.

"Said somethin' about some chick givin' 'im grief, and he wanted her taken care of." Jocko shrugged and pushed out a sloppy smoke ring that floated lazily in the night air before scattering. "He also said you were havin' trouble with it."

"What else?"

"That's about it."

Bill didn't like the way Baines had averted his eyes at that last statement. He'd heard several stories about how Frank handled his affairs.

160

Everyone knew full well that Frank detested disloyalty. He'd also heard that if Frank didn't think he could trust someone, they didn't stay too long on his payroll. He had to assume Frank trusted Jocko with this and told him to keep things as vague as possible and tell Bill just enough to get by.

It's them against me.

"You got somethin' to add?" Jocko was watching him.

"Not really." Bill decided to give Jocko the same treatment.

Jocko narrowed his eyes and stared directly at Bill. "What's your problem, by the way?"

Bill forced his mind to work on some sort of satisfactory explanation. Otherwise, Jocko would get suspicious and the war of wits would begin. He shrugged and decided on the macho approach. "Just don't like dusting females."

Jocko nodded and lit another cigarette. "Gotcha."

"Don't tell me *you* do," Bill said.

Jocko shrugged and pushed out a thick billow of gray smoke. "Don't matter none to me. When there's money involved? I kinda go with the dude handin' out the cash."

"Gotcha." Bill went back inside and forced his nerves to settle down. He'd wanted very much to strangle Jock Baines outside the club.

It was a damned shame he couldn't do it without getting himself in one helluva jam.

161

Chapter 16

"My story starts with my grandmother," Julie began.

"I take it she also had this gift you're going to tell me about?" Robert asked.

Julie could feel the warmth of the wonderful memories as the images returned, bringing with them her grandmother's beautiful smile as well as the lovely lady's bright aura. "She first told me about it when I was a little girl, but I was much too young to understand any of it at the time."

"When *did* you understand?"

She smiled when she recalled her grandmother's infinite patience as the lady tried so hard to explain their special gift. "I honestly don't think I'm quite there yet."

"But you obviously know a little more about it now, right?"

"It took a while, but yes, I guess you could say that."

"And what happened to help you understand it better?"

Julie could feel the warm tears gathering in her eyes. The vision of the graveyard came right back, along with the warmth she'd felt coming from her grandmother's stone, and then the butterfly settling on the rental car antenna, watching her before it flew away, floating gently just above the stone on its return to the pine forest. "When she died."

"When did it happen?" he asked softly.

"Last year, not long after my last visit to her place."

That sunny afternoon came right back, as if it had been in the very center of her memories. Julie could never forget that very pleasant stroll in the old woman's backyard and knew the memory would always be there, as if its bright image had been permanently etched into her spirit.

"This special gift will help you through life," Gram told her. "And if you don't ignore it or try pushing it away, it will protect you."

Julie couldn't help thinking that her grandmother was just trying to make her feel better. Julie had just told her about Nolan leaving her and the trouble she'd been having keeping her flower shop from going under.

She'd studied Bookkeeping and Accounting at UCF but hadn't been interested in working at a bank or any other large institution. She'd always wanted to work for herself and had gone into debt opening the shop in Winter Park. Business had been painfully slow at first, but her perseverance as well as her bright personality had eventually triumphed, and in just six months, the shop began running fairly well. The customers liked her, and in no time at all became return customers, and through word of mouth and a little local advertising, Julie's place had been able to remain in the green for the remainder of the year.

However, the trouble with Nolan had taken a toll on her emotionally, and it wasn't long before she noticed a definite drop in business. She knew something like this had to be directly related to her

163

emotional state and hoped she would soon be able to lift her spirits and get the shop thriving again.

She hated burdening her relatives with her problems. However, talking to Gram was different. She and her grandmother had always been very close. Julie loved staying with her during summer vacation, while she was in grade school and then in high school. She always found it difficult to reveal her innermost feelings to anyone, even Nolan, but she never had any problem opening up to her grandmother. The sweet lady had a special gift for making you want to share everything with her. And once you told her your most intimate secrets, everything suddenly looked brighter. You felt happier. Life had become much more exciting. You sincerely believed you possessed the ability to solve any problem that came your way.

This was what she was thinking when the dear lady told her about the gift. It happened the last time they'd visited her that last summer Dad and Mom had spent their vacation together. Julie had just turned eleven. At that age, however, she just couldn't quite grasp what her grandmother was trying to tell her.

She could remember only the strange darkness that had swept through her when something inside her told her that she shouldn't cross the highway. This was when she first realized something was very different about her. Something she couldn't quite explain. Something she had not seen in others. There had been quite a few other instances since, but since they'd all seemed minor, she dismissed them.

Last year, however, when Julie suspected that her grandmother was beginning to fail in her mental capacity, she didn't think she could believe much of what the old woman had told her about her gift.

"Why do we even have this gift?" she asked as they strolled down the crooked dirt path behind the big farmhouse. "What makes us so special?"

"Child, I've been trying to figure that one out all my life."

"Did you come up with anything?"

"Not really…"

"Nothing? At all?"

"All I can say is this. Maybe we really don't have to fully understand such wonders to appreciate them. I'm fairly certain the Almighty has a purpose for everything and everyone, and if He wanted us to know something, He would make sure something like that would happen. But as I just said, accept it and don't try fighting it or pushing it away. Accept it, believe it, and you'll never be sorry."

"Is it just a feeling? Like that darkness thing I felt when I was little?"

"With me, it always felt like someone who'd once been very close to me was right there beside me, guiding me along the right path."

"You mean, like an angel?"

Gram thought that over and nodded. "Maybe. I always thought it was one of our own, using their own special aura to shield us from the darkness and hatred in the world."

"Strange…" Julie liked the idea but thought it a bit over the top.

"It has always protected me, child…"

"Always?"

"Ever since I can remember."

"How? Did it…I mean, do you hear a voice?"

"Sometimes a voice, other times just a feeling. Like your darkness thing."

"I don't understand how I'm supposed to know if that's what it is, or what I'm supposed to do."

"It depends on the circumstance. But believe me, when it's there, you'll know what to do."

"When you hear the voice, do you recognize it?"

"Sometimes."

"Just sometimes?"

"The other times the voice sounds almost like my own."

Julie didn't know what to make of all this. It was very confusing. "I don't think I'll ever understand any of this."

"I don't think you really have to, child…"

"No?"

The old woman smiled. Her crinkly blue eyes, which had always been bright and beautiful, showed clear signs of the burden of many years. However, Julie would never forget the warmth that had always emanated from them and would treasure these special visits with much love. She would not know that this very special sunny afternoon would be the last time she would ever see that smile on her beloved grandmother's dear face.

"It's always been part of me, child," the woman replied after some thought. "It's been part of my happy moments, my sad ones, and has helped me overcome life's burdens and challenges. My

166

grandmother told me about it when I was about the same age you were when I first told you."

Julie still couldn't understand why her mother had never told her about such a thing. "My mother never told me about it. I guess this is why I never knew until you told me."

"Your momma didn't tell you 'cause she doesn't know very much about it."

"How can that be? If she has it, wouldn't she want to—"

"She doesn't have it, child. From what I was told, it skips a generation."

"What about my sister?"

"And for some reason no one seems to know, it only affects one child, usually the youngest."

"I'm the lucky one, then?"

"You most certainly are. And believe me, one day you'll know just how lucky you are because of it."

"Really?"

"It's just like having a tiny drop of sunshine in the palm of your hand."

Julie had no way of responding to that. It sounded much too fantastic.

"Child, my grandmother shared it with me just as I've shared it with you. It comes with love from my heart, and when something is given to you with that sort of love, its love grows and grows, and eventually becomes part of you. Cherish it as I have, and you will always be strong and capable of overcoming every obstacle life hits you with."

It comes with love from my heart...

Cherish it as I have…and you will always be strong…

A tiny drop of sunshine…

When the image popped into her mind the day she'd met Robert, Julie realized exactly what her grandmother was trying to tell her.

The image of her grandmother's beautiful, smiling face had blipped brightly in her mind the moment the strange voice in her head told her to get the cabby to stop the car.

***

"My grandmother was a great lady."

As always, Julie experienced sheer pleasure just by stating the obvious. "There was always something special about her."

Robert poured a cup of fresh coffee from the pot. "Are you talking about your gift? Or something else?"

Julie sugared her coffee and thought about something that would explain just how wonderful her grandmother really was. It didn't take her long at all to sum up the sweet lady with a simple image. "You've heard that old adage about someone lighting up a room, right?"

"A few times…"

"That described her perfectly. Whenever my grandmother came into a room, everything really did seem to brighten. She once told me that having this gift was like having a tiny drop of sunshine in your hand. It took me a little while to piece it together, but she was right. It seemed as if a special inner light followed her around, no matter where she went."

168

"I've read about people like that," he said. "Some seem to think there are people whose aura makes them very rare. Some even refer to them as white spirits."

"What do *you* think about all this?"

He seemed puzzled by her question. "It's not important what I think. All you need to know is—"

"Yes it is." She wanted very much to know everything he felt about her. "It's *very* important."

"Really?"

"To me, it is."

"Well, I have to admit that I was kinda overwhelmed by what happened on Semoran the other day…"

"I'm sorry, but if I hadn't done it—"

"Believe me, I'm grateful you did. Otherwise, we wouldn't even be sitting here."

"The three of us would be dead. Or in Intensive Care."

"And I'm sorry I didn't believe you when you told me it happened that way because you've got a sixth sense."

His statement surprised her. "You…didn't believe me?"

"Not entirely."

"I suppose that did sound a little…out there."

"I could tell something strange had happened, but I thought it was more than just a sixth sense sort of thing."

"What did you think it was?"

He had a sip of coffee. "This is gonna sound way over the top, but…"

"But what?"

He didn't reply.

"Please tell me. I really need to know what you think of me."

He gave her one of his smiles. "You should know how I think of you by now."

"I mean about *this*."

"It's that important to you?"

"It really is."

"Well, as I just said, this kinda goes way over the top, but what I can make out of it is that maybe your grandmother might have had a little extra help all her life."

"You mean, like from above?"

"I'm not sure I can make that call. I only know that there are things in this world, especially when dealing with the spiritual, that could explain many situations and mysteries we would never otherwise understand."

Julie had hoped Robert would understand what she was trying to tell him and not dismiss it entirely, as most others would. She realized how strange this concept was and how difficult it would be for others to try interpreting it. She wondered if she should tell Robert the rest of it. Part of her wanted him to know while the other part, the more practical, didn't want to burden him with too much of this at once. But when he said, "Tell me more about her," she felt a strong bond with this man and knew right then that it would be a grave mistake to keep anything from him.

"Well, as I just said, she was very special, and everyone she ever met could sense something unusual about her."

"They said that?"

"Not in so many words, but as Mom once told me, you could tell she had a positive effect on people by just being in their presence."

"How?"

"By the way their moods changed."

"Changed how?"

A particular incident popped up in her head the moment he asked the question. "One thing really stands out that I don't think I'll ever forget. It happened a couple of years ago when I was staying with her. I'd spend at least a week with her every summer, usually in June or July. She was having trouble with her freezer and called an electrician to stop by and see if he could look at the motor, or whatever wasn't functioning properly. Anyway, the man showed up a few hours later, and he was in a terrible mood. I was in the living room, watching TV when he came into the house, so I didn't actually hear or know what was going on when she led him into the laundry room, where she kept her freezer."

"How'd you know he was in a terrible mood?"

"I heard him talking. He had a really gruff voice, and as soon as he came in, I sensed a lot of tension and—"

"That's right, you've got this, too."

"Anyway, I talked to her after the man had left. She told me that his oldest son had been involved in a traffic accident and was lying in the hospital, recovering from terrible head trauma. He couldn't keep his mind on his work, and Gram felt badly about calling him out there when he should have

171

been in the hospital with his wife and son. He told her he needed to work to get his mind back on straight, and Gram told him that she had a very strong feeling his son was going to pull through."

"He believed her?"

Julie shrugged. "Of course."

"Did they know one another?"

"They'd never met before that day."

"Did you ever find out if she was right about the man's son?"

Julie smiled. "She said he called a few days later to tell her their son was doing just fine."

Robert shook his head. "Wow…"

"As I've already said, my grandmother had a way of looking at you and talking to you that made you feel good about everything. It didn't matter what was going on, or how bad you thought things were. Just a few moments with her and things seemed to brighten up. You just knew everything would turn out okay, because you had this strong feeling that she would never lie to you."

"I totally understand."

"How could you? You've never even—"

"I saw and felt the same thing when I first laid eyes on you."

172

DAY FOUR

Chapter 17

"You're clockin' out at two, right?"

Jocko Baines had come back inside and stopped a couple of feet behind him, looking like he was about to get laid. Bill could tell the man wanted to make some quick money and didn't care what he had to do to earn it.

Bill didn't want to talk to Baines about this, but he had no choice. Since there were only two shifts, Baines knew exactly when Bill would be leaving. Baines was obviously very excited and desperately wanted to do the job. Bill also suspected Frank had told Baines to make sure he was the one who killed the girl. Baines was a bully and had the reputation for being rough with the customers. He had a hair trigger temper and liked showing off his strength. "Yeah," he replied flatly.

"Where's this broad live?"

Bill wanted to turn around and walk away but knew he had to comply with what their boss had planned. And this meant keeping Baines in the loop. Otherwise, the man would call Frank and tell him Bill was being a problem.

"Winter Park," he told Baines.

"Got the address?"

"Yeah."

Baines glanced at his watch. "Half an hour. Meet ya out in back as soon as we clock out. Usin' your Charger?"

"Yeah."

Baines swatted him sharply on the back, then disappeared down the hall that led to the lap dancing areas.

Bill remained standing there, wondering what he could do to stop all this. Or at least get the girl out of harm's way.

Otherwise, she faced a very bleak—and extremely short—future.

***

At 1:00, Julie and Robert sat on the couch in the living room while *Casablanca* played on her widescreen.

After their talk in the kitchen, Robert had no idea how he should feel about Julie's story. It was only natural that she was troubled, but when he'd asked her if there was anything he could do to help, she'd said, "It's all right. Just sitting here with you, while my favorite movie is playing, is helping immensely."

"It's making you feel better?" He couldn't understand how watching a movie could rid her mind of something as serious and as frightening as the notion of being stalked.

She sighed deeply. "Now that the worst is over, I really think so."

"What do you mean by the worst?" Her reply confused him.

She didn't respond right off. He could tell something else had been bothering her. Moments later, she placed her hand on his thigh and smiled at him. "You're still here," she replied in a soft voice.

It took him a moment to realize what she'd meant. The very notion angered him, and he couldn't help thinking that anyone who would walk out on a girl like Julie for *any* reason could not possibly be in his right mind. "You actually thought that crap would scare me off?"

A nod.

"You still don't know me very well, do you?"

She smiled. "I think I'm getting there a lot quicker than I ever imagined possible."

"Personally, I think you're already there."

"You're mad at me?"

"Only because you thought I'd bail."

She moved closer. "Now I know for sure."

"Good, because I wouldn't."

"Ever?"

"Not in *this* lifetime."

They kissed.

After the kiss, Robert said, "I think we need to call someone."

"Whaddya mean?"

"Someone's after you. I don't want anything bad to happen to you, so I think we'd better let someone know."

"Like who?"

"Like maybe the cops."

"And tell them what?"

"How about telling them what you just told me?"

"I can't."

"Why not?"

175

"They'll want proof."

"How about the little guy who—"

"There's no proof."

"But—"

"There's really no way of tracking him down or even finding out who he is. The store doesn't have cameras. Besides, there are no witnesses. Gwen wasn't around at the time, and if there were any customers, they were probably milling around in another part of the store when he came in."

"I just think—"

"The car he was driving was probably an airport rental."

"What about—"

"The man I bumped into behind Schiller's?"

"No way of describing him?"

"I only got a glance. And it was dark."

"And you saw nothing else that night?"

"I have no idea what happened there."

"How about—"

"Or even where the big guy was going after I bumped into him."

He went silent. She had a point—several points. But that didn't change the fact that her life was in danger. And he had no intention of letting anyone hurt her.

"Do you own a gun?" he asked.

"What do *you* think?"

"Silly question, I guess…"

"How about you?"

"I've got a handgun back in my apartment."

"If you had it with you, would you use it?"

"That would depend."

"On what?"

"If I could get to it in time. It would probably be in the BMW, in the console, most likely."

She didn't reply.

Her silence told him just how hopeless this situation really was.

However, he had no intention of just sitting idly by.

"Julie—"

"I know what you're gonna say."

"I know that you know. Please humor me anyway."

She smiled. "You're gonna say what all guys would say. You're gonna turn super protective and tell me that you'll give them helluva fight, and that they won't know what hit them, and—"

"I wouldn't be much of a guy if I didn't at least *try* to protect you."

"Don't you realize that the bad men coming after me might be a little more than both you and I can handle?"

"I honestly don't care."

"That's very sweet, but—"

"Now you're gonna pull that emasculation thing on me that all women seem to know how to do, aren't you?"

"That's kind of harsh…"

"You're doing it very softly and gently, but it means the same thing, doesn't it?"

"I'm just trying to protect you."

"*You're* protecting *me*?"

"I'm just trying to let you know that I might be facing some very bad people."

"I know."

"People with attitudes."

"Probably."

"And guns."

"That, too."

"As I just said, it's very sweet of you to want to protect me, but—"

"You don't want me to get hurt?"

She sighed. "Well…"

"That's about it in a nutshell, right?"

She didn't reply.

They sat in silence for several long, uncomfortable minutes. Then Robert said, "Just answer this one very important question, okay?"

"All right…"

"If you won't let me try and protect you, how are you gonna protect yourself?"

"I'm not."

He didn't reply. He couldn't. There was nothing he could say about that. Did she intend to just sit there and let them do what they intended to do? And what about him? What did she expect him to do? Sit there beside her and watch?

This made no sense. None whatsoever.

He had to do something. He had no idea what he could do; he just knew he couldn't sit there and let some psycho do whatever he wanted to her. He couldn't live with himself if something like that happened.

Then, in the midst of his turmoil, she laughed and said, "You're kinda floored by what I just said, aren't you?"

"Extremely."

"You do believe me, don't you?"

"Actually, I have no idea *what* to believe."

"Then I'll explain it so you don't have to be beating yourself up anymore."

"I'd really appreciate it."

"I just said I'm not gonna protect myself."

"Yes. I remember."

"Know why I said it?"

"I wish I did, but no. I don't."

"I said it because it's the truth."

"Well, I assumed you wouldn't lie to me about something so obvious as that, but—"

"It *is* the truth. I have this very strong feeling that my gift will protect me."

Had he heard her right? Had she really said what he thought she said? "Are you sure about that?"

Her expression was deadly serious when she replied, "I'm sure."

***

"Why the hell are ya so bummed out about this?" Jocko Baines asked.

Bill made no comment as he took the Charger through the heavy crosstown traffic. He was having a rough time keeping his temper in check and didn't appreciate the gung-ho attitude Baines had been displaying for the last hour.

"You doin' the bitch or somethin'?"

Bill shot him a glare. He really hoped Baines would stop pushing the envelope. He didn't know how much more of this needling he could take.

"Well? Are ya? The way you're actin'? I'm not so sure you're bein' on the up and up."

179

"No. I'm not *doing* her."

Baines shook his head. "Gotta be *some* reason why you're actin' like a—"

"What exactly did Frank tell you? If he told you I've been seeing her, he's totally off base. I don't even know the lady. Hell, I've only seen her once. One time, and briefly."

"He didn't tell me that."

"What *did* he say?"

Jocko blew some cigarette smoke at the windshield. "Said some stupid chick stuck her nose in his business. He wants to make sure she don't open her mouth to the wrong people."

"That's it?"

Jocko sucked in more smoke. "Oh…and you're havin' a meltdown about doin' this, so ya needed help."

"Nothing else?"

Jocko shrugged. "What else do ya need to know? Frank's got his hands in some heavy shit. He don't need some nosy female makin' life harder. He always says a female oughta know when to open her mouth and when to keep it shut, right?" He snickered.

Bill didn't respond. He was still trying to figure out what he could do about Baines without getting into a dogfight with Frank. Things seemed hopeless, and even though he couldn't get the woman out of his head, he mentally cursed her for putting him in this position.

"Just remembered somethin' else," Baines said, flicking his spent smoke out the open window.

"What's that?"

"Frank wants proof."

"He wants *what*?"

"He wants me to email 'im a picture."

"Whatever for?"

"Maybe to make sure the chick's dead. Since you couldn't do it, he prob'ly wants proof that it's finally done…"

"A *picture*?" Bill couldn't believe any of this. "He actually wants a *picture*?"

"Yep. And don't worry." Baines tapped his shirt pocket. "Since you prob'ly won't have the stomach for it, I'll use mine."

Dammit, Bill thought, wincing at a sudden dull ache low in his gut.

Could this fiasco possibly get any worse?

***

When *Casablanca* ended, Robert kept his arm around Julie's shoulders as she carefully wiped her eyes with a Kleenex.

"You gonna be okay?"

She smiled through her tears. "I always cry at the end of this movie."

"I thought *I* was the silly one here."

She sniffed. "You are."

"But you're not?"

"Why am *I* silly? Because I cry at sad endings?"

"I thought this was a *happy* ending."

"You would."

"It wasn't?"

"Did Bogie get the girl?"

"No, but her husband did."

"That's beside the point."

181

Robert shook his head. "Whoever thinks women are more romantic than men obviously doesn't know what they're talking about."

Julie watched him curiously. She was almost certain that he would have shared her opinion of the ending. He did seem more sympathetic than the other men she'd known. Now she wasn't so sure, and she had to admit that it bothered her. "You don't think she should've stayed with him?"

"With who? Bogie? Or that Laszlow guy?"

She shook her head. Now she was thinking that he was playing with her again. She just wasn't in the mood to play right now and was angry with herself for putting on the movie so soon after their grim talk. She'd needed a distraction and thought her favorite movie would suffice, but now that it had ended, she found that the depression and the feeling of hopelessness that had plagued her before had quickly returned. "I don't know why we're even talking about this."

"Neither do I. Could this be classified as an argument?"

"I don't *think* so…" Now she was angry with herself for another reason. "Do *you*?"

"All I know is, even though we seem to disagree on the ending, I enjoyed watching it with you, and now I've got to use the bathroom." He got up, kissed her on top of the head, and took his empty glass to the kitchen.

As he went down the hall, Julie took her glass and bowl into the kitchen to clean up the dishes.

The moment she heard the bathroom door close, that same darkness that had nudged her earlier that day nudged her again. She nearly dropped the bowl just as she washed it off and placed it in the drainer.

What on earth was going on?

She stood tensely at the sink, letting her senses work. To calm herself, she closed her eyes. Darkness engulfed her. A moment later, the darkness turned gray. The gray gradually lightened, turning silvery. Then, just moments after that, two figures

(men)

appeared and grew more distinct as their images brightened in her thoughts.

They're coming for you, child...

The instant she heard the soft, familiar voice, one very important issue told her she needed to act quickly.

Her eyes shot wide open.

Robert!

She turned toward the doorway. "I've got to warn him!"

Without hesitation, she ran out of the kitchen and hurried down the hall.

Chapter 18

"That her BMW parked in front of the building? Next to the Nissan?"

Jocko Baines sounded irritated as Bill Torchia parked the Charger across the street from the girl's condo.

Bill checked his watch. 2:48. Two vehicles were parked in front of the two-story building—a black BMW and a tan Nissan Rogue. Frank had given Bill the girl's address he'd obtained from one of his many OPD contacts. Frank's contact had also supplied the make and model of the girl's car, which was the Nissan. The plate number matched, making this a done deal. Terrific. So far, this was good to go without a hitch—which was something Bill did not exactly want.

However, the black BMW parked beside the Nissan could make this go south very quickly. Bill knew nothing about it. He sincerely hoped the girl wasn't having company. Others involved—male or female—could turn this into chaos. The fact that it was nearly three in the morning might make their surprise visit somewhat easier.

Either way, Bill was extremely uncomfortable with the entire matter.

"She owns the Nissan." Bill grabbed his lockpicking kit from the console between the seats. He'd used the tools only a couple of times when he worked as a private detective shortly after returning from Iraq. He hated having to use them again but figured he didn't have much of a choice. In a major

184

condo development like this one, way too many people were wandering about and could get in the way.

"Be a real bummer if she's shacked up." Jocko shook his head. "Hate havin' to put away some poor bastard just when he's gettin' his rocks off. But it's late, so they're prob'ly both sacked out." He gazed at the building. "Condo looks dark. Should be easy."

Bill said nothing. His thoughts raced. He'd heard what Baines had just said but didn't want to think about that for even a second. He was much too distracted trying to think of some way out of this without Baines pulling his macho shtick and gumming up everything.

"Guess we just sneak in." Jocko sounded pensive.

"I guess so…" Bill was thinking of alternatives.

"If they both just got off, they'll be easy to take care of. They won't even know what's goin' on while we're tyin' 'em up."

"We don't even know if she's got company in the first place." Bill was getting tired of Baines' crudeness.

"Okay, okay… Take it easy. Let's say she's alone. It'll be much easier, takin' care of a female who's half asleep. Even if she wakes up in the middle of it, she won't be much of a problem."

Bill didn't like the sound of that. "What are you talking about now?"

Baines pulled something out of his back pocket. It was a white cloth enclosed in a baggie.

"What the hell is *that*?" Bill could feel the back of his neck growing warm.

"Let's just say it'll make the babe go beddy-bye in twenty seconds."

"Chloroform? Seriously?" Bill couldn't believe this.

"Your momma didn't raise no idiots, did she?" Baines returned the packet to his pocket and shifted in his seat.

"Who gave that to you?"

"Who d'ya think?"

Bill rubbed his temples. Apparently Frank was taking no chances. Bill knew right then that he had to get Baines' mind off the rough stuff. He didn't want to go that route. If they did, there was no turning back.

"Makes things simple." Baines snapped his fingers. "We go on in, she's asleep?" He shrugged. "I juice 'er, then we bundle 'er up and take 'er out to the car. There's someone in there with 'er? He gets the beddy-bye treatment, too. No problem."

Bill glared. "You've seen too many bad mob movies. What makes you think she's even going to put up a struggle?"

"Think she's just gonna wake up, see the two of us in her bedroom, and not freak?"

Bill hated to admit Baines was right.

"We gotta sneak in and make sure she's out—which is why I brought along the juice. She wakes up early? We gotta keep 'er from screamin' and gettin' the neighbors involved. She needs somethin' to keep 'er quiet while I dose her up." He pulled what looked like a Sig Sauer out of his waistband.

"This keeps 'er quiet. I brought this in case she freaks out, big-time." With his other hand, he produced a silencer from his side pocket.

Bill stiffened in his seat. "You're *not* going to use that!"

"Have ya seen all these blue-haired assholes walkin' around? Whaddya think they'll do if they hear a gunshot?"

Bill turned in his seat and quickly scanned their surroundings. "It's three in the morning. I don't see anyone around. The elderly usually don't stay up this late."

"And what happens if one of 'em comes down the walk 'cause he can't sleep? He sees us carryin' her out to the car, he might just ask questions. You cap one of these assholes, you can't just leave 'em lyin' there, ya know…"

Bill began growing more and more uneasy. Baines was much too eager. It made him wonder if what Frank had really told him was something totally different from what Baines had told Bill. Since Frank Baroni was not known to be very honest, Bill clearly knew the answer to that. Besides, the chloroform told much of the story. "Let's just play this by ear and see where that goes."

"Seriously?"

"We might not have to threaten her with the gun at all."

"And if she freaks?"

"We'll worry about that when and if it happens."

"It'll happen, believe me."

"How can you be so damned sure about that?"

"Chicks freak when ya point a gun at 'em. I've done it at least half a dozen times. Guess what? They've freaked each time."

Bill ignored that last remark. "Maybe this one won't."

Baines shook his head.

"Like I said, we've got to play this by ear."

"And if that don't work?"

Bill sighed. "Then—and only then—we might have to get rough."

Baines chuckled. "'Bout damn time ya said somethin' that made sense!"

"I just don't think we'll need the chloroform."

"Either way, I got it with me." Baines slipped the Sig back in his waistband and the silencer back into his pocket. "We still don't know if she's alone. And if she ain't, I don't wanna have to waste any time roughin' up a dude if I don't have to. Especially when I can just knock 'im out, do the girl, and haul her away. We don't want this to take too long, ya know. Frank's expectin' to see what we did, and we both know he hates to be kept waitin'."

Despite his fears, Bill felt somewhat relieved when he no longer saw the pistol in Baines' hand.

"*You're* packin', ain't ya? Besides that lockpickin' shit, I mean."

"I always do."

"Okay, then…"

Bill's next thoughts came to him long before he expected them to. They were dark images, and they scared him. And disgusted him. It made him wonder what had really happened to him in Iraq, when he was forced to be an interrogator.

"Well?"

Baines' voice snapped him out of his nightmare. It pulled him away from the bloody past but brought him back to the present. "Well what?"

Baines was staring at him. "Like I said, we don't have too much time. Besides, my ass is gettin' numb, warmin' up the damn seat."

"All right, then." Suddenly angry, Bill pushed open his door. "Let's get this over with."

***

"Whaddya mean, I have to leave?"

Standing in the bathroom doorway, Robert gawked at Julie as she faced him in the hall. Her eyes were even bigger than normal. Fear. And terror. Both qualities showed clearly on her face, and it scared him. Something had terrified her during the last five minutes.

He thought of the incident earlier that day, and her reaction when he'd asked her about it. She'd shrugged it off, mumbling something about her mood swing.

But he knew better. Something had frightened her and knocked her right off her game. And now something—quite possibly the very same thing—was frightening her again. It apparently had something to do with her "gift," as she'd called it. The times he'd caught her reading his mind had suddenly become very clear, as well as the incident in the cab that had saved their lives. He knew full well that whatever was frightening her was very real. It also told him that he should be taking this very seriously.

189

"Tell me what's wrong." He placed his hands gently on her shoulders and immediately felt her trembling.

"I-I *can't*…"

"I promise I'll understand. Whatever it is, I'll understand. I might even be able to help."

"Robert—"

"Does this have anything to do with those people who could be after you? If I'm right, let me in on this, okay? Let me help you handle it. I honestly think I can. At least let me try. I'll call the police and—"

"*Please* don't question me, Robert…"

"I *have* to question you. I can't possibly leave while you're feeling this way. For one thing, not knowing what's going on would kill me. Can you imagine how I'll feel if I leave right now, while you're in this fragile state, and something bad happens to you? I'd *never* be able to forgive myself!"

"*Please* leave, Robert. I strongly sense something bad is—"

"I don't care."

"What?"

"If something bad is gonna happen to you, it's also gonna happen to me."

"But all you have to do is—"

"All I have to do is leave? Is this what you're trying to say?"

She just sighed and looked down at her feet.

"And if I leave, everything will turn out just fine? Whatever's frightening you will just vanish? No one will come after you? You'll sigh in relief,

190

fix your hair and makeup, then grab your cell and tell me to drive right on back because everything's okay and wonderful again?"

She reached up and patted her hair. "What's wrong with my hair?"

"This isn't exactly the right time for levity, you know…"

She sighed heavily. "I know…"

"And to get back to what we were talking about… As I just said, if I leave and something happens, this will haunt me for the rest of my life."

"Robert, this has nothing to do with you."

"If it involves you, it involves me. It took me a long, long time to find you, and I intend to hold on to you as long as I possibly can."

"Robert…"

He pulled her close. "As long as I'm with you, everything feels right, and even though something could—"

Just then, they heard the front door opening.

Julie spun around and gasped.

Keeping close to her, Robert moved out into the hall.

Two huge, broad-shouldered men had entered the apartment and were standing in front of the open door.

One held a gun aimed directly at them.

A silencer was attached to it.

Chapter 19

Just as he eased open the front door, Bill Torchia saw them standing out in the dimly lit hall, fully dressed, not twenty feet away.

His spirits sank. Not only was the girl not asleep in her bed, but she also had company!

This was not going to end well *at all*.

Jocko Baines had already pulled out his gun and silencer and aimed it directly at the two in the hall. Bill could tell Baines clearly wanted to use it.

Bill quickly closed the door. He tapped Baines on the forearm to remind him not to lose control, but Baines ignored him. He was clearly focused on the man and woman and noticed nothing else.

Bill knew that if either of the two made the slightest move, Baines would do the dirty deed right here. The silencer would keep the noise down, but the cleanup—as well as the bundling up and transport of the bodies—would be troublesome and time-consuming. It wouldn't be long at all before law enforcement and their forensics team showed and began sniffing around for clues.

Bill had to step in and take control. Otherwise, Baines would turn this into a bloodbath. He needed to keep his wits about him and make sure the situation didn't automatically explode.

Right now, things were as tolerable as possible considering the circumstances. Neither the woman nor the man had fallen into panic mode. They were obviously frightened, but this was to be expected. Right now, they were standing perfectly still, their hands raised while concentrating on Baines' gun. The man's expression, as well as his stiff posture, suggested that he was more frightened than the woman. She stared unflinchingly at Baines and seemed strangely calm. Bill wondered if she had already gone into shock.

A moment later, she said, "If you've come to rob us—"

"Shuddup!" Baines' harsh whisper was venomous. "Don't move, and nobody'll get hurt."

"What do you want?" The man was frightened but seemed to be in control. "And how'd you get in? I distinctly remember locking the door." He turned to the girl. "You didn't unlock the door, did you?"

She frowned. "Why would I? I *always* keep the door locked. You just never know when something bad is gonna happen. Like what's happening right now."

"You're right. This would be a great example of what can happen even when you're careful…"

As he spoke, the man shifted slightly toward his left, shielding the girl from the direct line of fire. Bill gave him a couple of dozen points for risking his own skin to protect her. And gave the two of them several more dozen points for talking calmly to one another with a loaded gun pointed directly at them.

"I guess I should've put the chain on the door," the woman said. "Then maybe this wouldn't have—"

"I said, *shuddup*! And *don't fuckin' move*!" Baines sounded like he was barely holding it together. Bill guessed that it was because they

193

weren't acting scared enough. Baines might throw caution to the wind and use the gun just to show superiority. "Move only when I tell ya to. Otherwise, just stand there, and we'll all—"

"Everyone just please *relax*..." Bill was growing tired of Baines' inflated bravado. He didn't want this to escalate. The silenced gunshot would certainly not be loud enough to alert the complex. However, there would still be a mess to clean up, and Bill wasn't sure he could eradicate all signs of Baines and himself being there.

He had to think of something very quickly...

***

They've come to take you away, child...

The voice was soft but very clear, yet Julie could sense right off that the man on her left, the good-looking one, did not want to be here in the first place.

She remembered seeing him once before. He was the man who'd come into her office and stood in the doorway, staring at her, then spun around seconds later and rushed out of the shop.

The one holding the gun seemed to be enjoying himself. The darkness of his aura showed clearly in the semidarkness of the living room. She could almost feel the tension his finger had on the trigger of the gun and hadn't liked it one bit when Robert shifted his position to shield her.

She could deal with that later. Right now, she was much too concerned about the reasoning for this violent intrusion.

This was it, wasn't it? She knew they were coming for her, and now they had proven her right.

This was all about the big, mean-eyed guy she'd crossed paths with six weeks earlier. He had done something horrible, and since she had seen him, he considered her a nuisance, a problem.

They want me to disappear.

The one holding the gun seemed hellbent on using it. The other guy didn't appear as threatening, but Julie didn't think he would be able to stop his partner from shooting her and Robert.

If she could somehow coax the gun out of the picture, she might be able to reason with them.

"I've seen you before," she told the good-looking one.

His partner glanced at him and mumbled something.

"You came to my shop, didn't you?"

After some hesitation, he nodded.

"Why are you here?" she asked the one holding the gun.

The gun twitched slightly in his hand. "I didn't say you could talk, bitch," he muttered, glaring.

She felt Robert stiffen. Since he was standing in the direct path of the man's gun, she had to be very careful about her reactions.

"I'm sorry, lady," the good-looking guy said in a soft, gentle voice, "but you and your friend are gonna have to come with us."

"Now why would we want to go anywhere with you?"

His partner practically cringed at the sound of her voice. "I told ya to shut up and—"

She focused on the man's deep-set, glaring eyes and imagined his aura lightening. "I really wish you wouldn't talk to me like that. You're not being very nice, you know…"

He opened his mouth to say something and stopped. His glare disappeared, and he groaned.

"Please," the other man said. "If you'll just do as we say—"

She could sense his fear. His heart was not into this. All she had to do was keep her eyes on him and his aura would lighten. In a soft voice she said, "Do you *really* want to take us somewhere? Really and truly? You're not *really* gonna *hurt* us or anything, are you?"

He shook his head and stared at the floor, then looked around as if he were checking his surroundings. When his gaze settled on her and Robert, he squinted as if noticing them for the first time.

Julie focused on him again, then his partner, and visualized their auras lightening even more. *You really don't want to be here, do you?* she asked them both, using her inner voice. *You don't even know why you're here, do you?*

The mean-looking one stopped staring at her and regarded his gun for a few moments. Just then, his arm dropped to his side.

Julie sensed fear emanating from him. He turned to his partner. Both were thinking the same

(what are we doing here?)

thoughts, and the situation became quite clear.

Julie couldn't just let them return to their employer with this hanging over their heads. She suspected something very bad would happen to them if they didn't accomplish what they were told

196

to do. She knew she couldn't live with herself if she let this happen.

Then she wondered why she should feel even a little responsible for two men who had broken into her place with plans to take her somewhere and kill her.

I don't know. I just do.

There is only one way for you to handle this, child, the inner voice said.

Yes. I know.

Julie visualized the mean-looking one putting his gun away.

An instant later, he removed the silencer. He then shoved his gun back into his waistband and the silencer in his side pocket.

His partner seemed to relax, but when he saw his partner making a move for his back pocket, he whispered, "*No.*"

The other man sighed and let his arm drop to his side.

"I'll go with you," Julie said, "but Robert stays here."

"Julie?" Robert's exasperated expression told her he didn't like what she'd just said. "I can't let you leave with them alone and—"

"I'll be okay."

"But *I* won't be. I just can't let you—"

"You're not *letting* me, Robert. I'm doing this on my own."

"But—"

"No buts."

The good-looking one frowned.

She focused on him and said very softly, "You'll both feel very, very bad if you bring him with us and something happens to him…"

Both men said nothing.

"Julie…"

"Trust me, okay?"

He continued staring.

She focused on his beautiful chestnut eyes. "Please?"

He shrugged loosely. "I guess I've got no choice."

She smiled and kissed him lightly on the lips. "I'll be back before you've even realized you've missed me."

He returned her smile. It was weak and showed some fear, but it still made her feel very warm inside. "In that case, you're already late."

She kissed him again. "Anyway, I've got to come back and finish *that*."

"Finish what?"

She moved closer. "That kiss, silly."

"It *was* sort of flimsy…"

"Not exactly my best work?"

"Nowhere near."

"I'll make up for it."

"You'd better."

"Is that an order?"

"Damned straight."

Chapter 20

Racked with confusion, Bill Torchia slid behind the wheel of the Charger. The girl, Julie, got in the seat beside him while Jocko Baines climbed in back.

Bill had no idea what the hell had just happened. Frank's orders were simple: sneak into the girl's condo, put out her lights, then drive her out in the woods and dump her. Just make sure you email him a pic as proof that you did the deed.

However, there was a guy in the picture—which complicated things. He was in the condo with the girl, and the two were standing out in the hall when Bill and Baines went inside. They were watching them as Bill pushed the front door open and followed Baines inside—

Wait a minute...

He glanced at her, then shifted in his seat to have a look at the backseat. Baines was sitting there, looking as stupid as usual, his eyes glazed and off-center.

Sitting alone.

Baines was in back, sitting alone. Just the girl and Baines. And, of course, Bill in the driver's seat.

Something was very wrong. There should be four, but there weren't. There were only three. Bill, the girl, and Baines.

Where the hell was the guy?

Why did the girl come out by herself?

Was this her idea or his? Why couldn't he remember?

It didn't matter whose idea it was because none of this made any sense. There were *three* in the Charger—not *four*. Both the guy and the girl should be in the car with them.

For some reason, nothing that should have happened had actually happened. The girl wasn't in her bed, asleep. It was three in the morning, but instead of being asleep in her bed, she was standing out in the hall with a guy, and both were fully dressed. For another, they—

Something else had taken place. Something totally different. Something extremely weird.

What the hell was it?

He tried piecing it all out, but nothing made sense. Every time he thought he'd reached a conclusion, his head turned cloudy and he forgot what he was thinking about.

Had *she* done this? If so, how?

Did it have anything to do with those incredible blue eyes? Was there something about them that hypnotized whoever they were focused on and made a guy do all sorts of weird, screwy things?

Was it even possible to get other people to do weird, screwy things just by looking at them?

Strange… This seemed just like something out of one of those horror flicks.

"We're not going to sit here much longer, are we?" she asked.

Her voice made him jerk in his seat.

She was right; they had to get out of there. And they had to do it soon, because…because…

For some reason that just wouldn't become clear, he couldn't remember why they had to get out of there.

Bill buckled his seat belt and watched as she buckled hers.

Just as he started the car and began backing out of the space, she said, "Where are you taking me?"

That was a good question. He tried focusing once again, but his thoughts immediately went all sideways and fuzzy. Something about taking her somewhere, right? Wasn't that what she'd just asked?

How could he possibly forget something the girl asked when she asked the question just seconds ago? Was he getting Old Timer's already? Too many damned punches to the head from the cage fighting? Or had he been hit with more shrapnel from that IED than they managed to find and pull out after they brought him in to the hospital?

Where are you taking me?

That was it. Well, wasn't it? And if it was, what would the answer be?

A sudden flash of the club brightened in his head.

The club? Why would he suddenly be thinking about the club?

Because of Frank, of course. Frank was sitting in his office, waiting to hear from them. And he was going to be pissed because Bill had no idea what to tell him.

"Well? Aren't you going to tell me?"

That was a very good question. Where *were* they taking her?

201

It had something to do with the woods, didn't it? Wasn't that where Frank had wanted them to take her? Or was that just another hairbrained idea Baines had thought up?

He had no idea. His thoughts were cloudy. He began wondering if Iraq was somehow creeping back to him so it could take over again.

I can't let that happen again. I just can't!

You're gonna be all right...

Bill shivered as cold tingles trickled down his spine.

Where the hell had *that* voice come from?

Whose voice was it? It certainly wasn't his own, and for a moment he wondered if it belonged to a female.

A female's voice in his head? How weird was *that*?

And what the hell did that have to do with this girl and where they were taking—

"You're taking me to your boss, aren't you?"

His hands gripped the wheel so tightly that his fingers quickly went numb. Once again he wondered how she'd just done that. How she had jumped right in there, as if she had been listening to whatever had been happening in his head.

You're taking me to your boss...

He struggled to remember if he had actually talked to her about that, but all that registered was the fact that he and Baines weren't under any circumstances supposed to bring her to the club *at all*. Just why this woman wanted to talk to Frank was a total mystery. The only thing Bill could think

202

of was that if he and Baines brought her to Frank's office, they'd both be toast in record time.

"We *can't* take you to see him," Bill said softly.

"Why not?" she asked.

"The boss won't like it," Jocko said from the back seat.

She turned around. "Is this what he told you?" she asked him.

"H-Huh? Uh, yeah…" Baines didn't sound convincing.

"Do *you* agree?" she asked Bill.

He didn't reply. He gritted his teeth as his nerves began to quiver.

"Where does he want you to take me, then?"

Bill couldn't reply. Neither could Baines.

Bill could feel those eyes on him again.

"Were you going to take me somewhere out in the middle of the woods, by any chance?"

Bill felt his nerves quivering even worse. It was getting more difficult to keep his hands fastened to the steering wheel.

How the hell did she know *that*? How the hell could she possibly know what they'd planned to do?

Was she reading their minds?

How could anyone read someone else's mind?

He tried once again to recall what had been said in her condo, but once again, his mind clouded over and nothing would come. He could remember picking the lock and opening the front door. Seeing them standing there, watching Bill and Baines as they came in. Baines pointing his gun. The girl and someone else—that guy who was with her, maybe?—standing there, watching them with their hands up. Then—

Everything else turned into a blur.

"I hope you won't mind," she said, sounding somewhat cryptic, "but there's been a change of plans."

A change of plans? What the hell is she talking about?

"Wh-What?" He strongly suspected something else was about to happen. He feared it was something neither he nor Baines would appreciate.

"I really need to talk to him," she said. "Your boss."

"Huh?" His hands slipped on the wheel. The Charger nearly bumped the small pickup in the lane beside them. Why in heaven's name would she insist on talking with Frank Baroni?

"Your boss. I think we should be going there right now. There are things he needs to know. Things he doesn't seem to understand."

"No can do, lady!" Baines sounded exasperated. "We're not even s'posed to be takin' you to see him. He'll have a shit fit if—"

"Where's your boss right now?"

Baines didn't respond.

The girl turned to Bill. "Where is he?"

Bill could feel the intensity of those eyes once again. His resolve began crumbling. He knew that he had to tell her the truth. "At the...c-club," he said nervously.

"That's where we're going, then."

Bill had to reason with her. They *couldn't* take her to see Frank. They just *couldn't*. He'd freak, and with his colossal temper, he'd have *all three* of them taken somewhere and dumped. "L-Listen, l-lady—"

"Please call me Julie."

"Listen, la—"

"Julie."

"Er, J-Julie, you don't know…what you're asking—"

"We have to see him, and you two know why."

Silence.

"You really don't want to kill me, do you?" she asked in a lighter tone.

More silence.

Bill found that his palms were sweating freely, making the steering wheel cover damp and slippery.

"Well?"

Bill began thinking of Puddles again. The sweet little guy his brother brought home after school, when Bill was just a little guy himself. The same cute puppy Bill had vowed to protect with his own life. For some strange reason, he was feeling the very same thing right now.

What the hell is happening to me? This isn't a cute little puppy, but a grown woman. How in heaven's name can I possibly compare the two?

Julie turned to Baines. "How about *you*? You don't want to kill me, do you?"

Silence.

She kept staring at Baines. Bill knew it was only a matter of time before the big brute crumbled.

Just then, he stammered, "N-nope…no can do…"

"All right, then. You've got to take me to see him so I can square it with you two."

A heavy silence.

"Everyone okay with this?"

More silence.

"You don't want this hanging over your heads, do you?"

Neither responded.

"I can do this, you know."

Silence.

"Look at it this way. You two came to my place to do something bad to me, but I convinced you not to. Neither of you saw that coming, did you?"

Bill could certainly not argue about that. The girl was absolutely right. And even though he had no idea how she'd done it, the fact that she had was more than enough to make his head spin.

"Well? Did you?" she asked Bill.

He shook his head.

"Nope," Baines mumbled.

"Good. It's settled, then."

Bill swallowed loudly. This would not go well at all. It was bad enough that he couldn't do the job the first time. But now this? Taking her to see Frank when Frank specifically told him to dump her somewhere and take pictures of the nasty deed?

His temples throbbed as he heard himself whispering, "He's not gonna like this. Not at all…"

"Oh, he won't mind."

Bill kept gazing at the road ahead and thought, *He's gonna have our hides. All three of us.*

"Believe me. He'll go along with this. Eventually." She sat back in her seat and stared straight ahead.

He's gonna kill us. I know he is.

"No, he's not," she said with a smile.

Bill glanced at her and trembled.

What the fuck? How the hell can she do that?

What have we gotten ourselves into?

He glanced at her once more.

Still smiling, Julie sat very relaxed, staring straight ahead.

Bill turned back to the road ahead and felt slightly less tense. For some strange reason, he had a funny feeling that things could turn out okay.

***

Robert parked the BMW in the front lot of BABES APLENTY as the Charger disappeared behind the big building.

He had no idea what was going on. When Julie decided to leave with the two thugs, she hadn't said what was on her mind. He could tell she'd somehow manipulated the two men but still couldn't figure out where this was going. He was afraid they would suddenly remember what they were supposed to do and then go through with their original plan. Fearful for her safety, he'd gotten into the BMW and, thanks to the steady early morning traffic, followed at a safe distance.

The two men looked like bouncers—which gave him some idea why they'd brought her here. Based on what Julie had told him earlier, the man behind all this could be the owner or manager of the club. Robert had heard from several sources that this place, as well as CLUB VENUS, was owned by the mob and had close connections with local politicians. The one she had bumped into that night could have been any one of them.

What really mattered was that Julie could be in mortal danger, and Robert had no intention of letting anything happen to her. He was falling in love with her and was convinced she was falling for him as well. And this, more than anything, assured him that protecting her was his one and only option.

His nerves shook as he got out of the BMW, but he ignored the feeling and concentrated on finding Julie and bringing her back to her condo. He had no plans other than going inside and looking for her. He kept reminding himself that Julie had quite a few tricks of her own and could handle herself in tense situations. He knew full well that the two who'd broken into her place had originally intended to kill her. However, judging by their strange behavior just before they'd left the condo, he guessed that she had somehow changed their gameplan. Why they'd brought her here was anyone's guess. He trusted her judgment and was confident in her strange abilities but knew he couldn't rest until he found her.

His legs slightly unsteady, he went up the steps leading to the two-story pink stucco building, where a pair of huge, broad-shouldered men in loose-fitting suits waited for him to give them the club's cover charge.

***

Sitting tensely behind the wheel of the Charger, Bill Torchia stared at the rear door of the club and wanted to disappear.

He groaned and gently rubbed his temples. He really didn't want to go through with this. Despite what Julie had promised them, he knew damned well that he and Jocko Baines were in serious trouble the instant they brought her into Frank's office.

Frank wanted her dead—*not* wandering around in his club, and certainly not showing up in his office.

He just couldn't understand why he and Baines had brought her here in the first place. He also tried to figure out the moment when he realized he wasn't going to do what he and Baines were ordered to do.

But as hard as he tried, he just couldn't nail it down. This woman had somehow taken charge of the situation the moment they'd gone into her condo, and nothing they could have said or done would have changed a damned thing.

He still couldn't stop thinking about what had happened on the way over.

He's gonna kill us, he'd thought dismally. *I know he is.*

"*No, he's not*," she'd said, her smile telling him that she had actually read his thoughts.

She knows, he kept telling himself. *She actually knows what's gonna happen!*

Was she a witch? One of those psychics he'd read about as a kid?

Or was this mind control?

Didn't matter. The only thing that really concerned him was the fact that they hadn't done what Frank had ordered them to do. And to make the situation even worse, they were about to take the girl into his office.

With a deep sigh, he turned to the rear door of the club and, looking at it, realized that this would probably be the last time he and Jocko would ever be able to use it.

"Are we going to sit out here all night?" she asked, startling them both. "Or are you gonna let me go inside and talk to your boss?"

Talk to your boss.

The girl turned around in her seat. "Are you ready to go in, too?"

Silence. Bill could tell Baines was thinking the very same miserable thoughts.

"It won't be that bad," she said softly.

Bill wanted to object, but once again she seemed to have read his thoughts. "Trust me." Smiling at him, she pushed her door open, then turned and swung her long legs out onto the gravel. "C'mon. I don't have all night."

The fear heavy in his gut, Bill pushed open his door and forced his tense body out of the Charger.

***

Robert squeezed through the heavy crowd.

As usual, the place was doing a bang-up business. It took him several minutes to reach the bar after he'd paid his cover at the door. The big room reverberated with choppy sounds of pop music blasting from the p.a. system. The long-haired, half-naked pole dancers performed their

210

sensuous routines on the counter of the long, U-shaped bar that ran from one end of the room to the other. Just beyond the end of the bar, three carpeted steps led to a different level that disappeared behind the wide archway. *Lap Dancing*, applied with square white stencils on a square black sign, sat on a short brass post in front of the wall.

Robert ordered a Manhattan and sat down on a barstool. While he waited, he checked out the activity in the big room. Small clots of well-dressed middle-aged guys struggled to be heard over the blaring sound system. Three slender waitresses in skimpy bras and panties dodged groping hands while whisking through the gaps in the crowd.

Since he'd been in strip clubs before, Robert saw nothing out of the ordinary. A high-class strip club doing booming business during the weekend. Nothing new here, right?

Wrong. *Dead* wrong, in fact, since Julie had been brought here by two bouncers in a Charger. And since these brutes had broken into Julie's condo an hour earlier, Robert found that he was even more suspicious about this place.

What were his options? Approach a waitress and ask one or two incriminating questions? How about the bargirl? The barman working with her?

Choices like that would not only be a big mistake, but it would also be extremely stupid. And dangerous, as well. It might even get him thrown out of the place. Or worse.

But what else could he do?

His drink came. He sampled it and was grateful it was strong. Only one of these for this trip would

211

be necessary. Otherwise, he'd get drunk. How could he find out anything about Julie if he sat here like an idiot, getting soused and sloppy?

How would this help Julie?

How would it help either of them?

A vacant table awaited him toward the rear, next to a maroon curtain that separated the room from another room. He paid for the drink, got down off the stool, went over to the table, and sat down facing the bar.

From where he sat, he had a clear picture. He decided to stay here for a while and plan some sort of strategy. He didn't think he could do much unless he saw one or both men who had broken into Julie's condo. If this happened, he could follow the brute— or brutes—and hope the trail would eventually lead to Julie's whereabouts. Otherwise, he would have to improvise and find out what sort of trouble he could get into. He sincerely hoped that if he did cause a fuss, it would earn him a meeting with the big man. Then he might be able to find out what happened to Julie and where she was before they tossed him out.

He decided to wait half an hour. If nothing happened, he'd use his cell and try her number. If she didn't respond, that would be clear evidence that she was in trouble. Then he could decide if he should call the cops or do whatever he could to disrupt the works enough where he'd be noticed.

He had to find her. He knew he couldn't rest unless he'd determined she was safe.

Until that happened, all bets were off.

Chapter 21

Frank Baroni had not been having a good evening.

For one thing, he hadn't heard from Torchia or Baines.

Both Torchia and Baines were good men, although Torchia hadn't been quite up to the task lately, since he'd screwed up that rush job with the brunette. Baines, however, wasn't exactly the shrinking violet type, and would deliver when push came to shove. Unless Torchia's laid-back approach infected Baines in some weird way, the job would get done, and Frank should be receiving pics of the happy event on his cell any time now.

This sort of bullshit shouldn't even be happening in the first place. Torchia was a damned *Marine*, for God's sake. He did a full tour in Iraq, and from what Frank had learned from the man's record, Torchia had saved the lives of several of his men and was responsible for eliminating nearly a dozen enemy insurgents. In his case, there was no need to be squeamish about planting one in the back of the head of a troublesome broad, was there?

Baines hadn't served, but that didn't matter— not one damned bit. He did time ten years or so ago for nearly destroying two Cuban gang members stupid enough to try and rob the big oaf when he was coming out of a liquor store just a few miles south of Miami Beach. The Cubans were big, armed with switchblades, hyped up on meth, and full of unbridled attitude. Baines, however, having spent

213

three years competing in bodybuilding contests, had been taking HGH and a list of other muscle enhancers and strength builders, and had no intention of handing over his bourbon or his wallet.

The case should have been classic self-defense. At face value, two armed, spaced-out gang members assaulting one unarmed man sounded ridiculously simple. But it didn't help Baines at all that during the scuffle, one of his attackers lost eight teeth, his left eye, and needed to have his jaw wired shut, or that the other had suffered a broken nose, six fractured ribs, a broken collarbone, and a severe concussion. To make the situation even worse, the DA had been running high on a serious war-on-crime campaign and decided that it would play better with the public to give Baines a few years in the genpop to reconsider his senseless act of uncontrolled brutality.

Baines was not exactly the type to develop a case of nausea or depression over capping someone—not even a good-looking female. Especially when two K in extra spending money awaited him.

As if that in itself wasn't enough to keep Frank's juices flowing hot, the old man had called three different times during the last twelve hours, wanting to know if Frank had spoken with their attorneys regarding the new fines the club had been facing for a number of different violations. Some were minor annoyances, such as rezoning issues. The others, mainly crime concerns, would put excessive pressure on Frank and the old man to address these fears as well as pad a bunch of deep pockets.

The old man could be a notorious butthole when facing pressure from state officials or politicians. He hated being pressured and hated it even worse when it looked like he'd have to spend a good deal of his valuable time sitting in a room with a bunch of grossly overpaid buttholes in fancy suits, playing the bargaining scheme that would most certainly cost both the old man and Frank more money than they cared to part with.

But that was the game and they both had been fully aware of it from the start. The old man had started his businesses in Brooklyn before moving down to Miami to open a string of clubs and bars. He knew what he was getting into down there, but eventually grew tired of their stupid politics. He relocated to Central Florida, bringing two of his favorite clubs with him. And since the political climate appeared more favorable in Orange County, he expected more wiggle room than he'd been getting.

This business with the nosy brunette could not have come at a worse time. It was bad enough that he'd had to personally cap Morgan Betz, the asshole who'd been stonewalling him with the liquor license fiasco that nearly got the Feds sniffing around for something they could use to close them down. But when this bitch showed up just a few yards away from where Frank had dropped Betz in the alley behind Schiller's Steakhouse, Frank knew his ass would be in a serious bind if things went sideways and the bitch opened her big mouth about seeing him there. Like his old man, Frank had made more than his share of enemies. He knew damned well that if word got out and the media learned that he'd been anywhere near Schiller's during Betz's murder, every damned newshound in the entire state would want his ass over a spit.

Frank poured some Scotch from the bottle and drank it right down. The bottle was already halfway gone. Hell, he'd just unsealed the damned thing two hours earlier, draining both its neck and shoulders in less than half an hour. At this rate, he'd be so shitfaced, he'd have to head home and put up with the wife screaming in his ear for the rest of the weekend. He needed to be stone sober when those two idiots finally reported in again.

Just then, someone knocked on the door.

Frank glanced at his watch. 4:30. Not exactly the best time of the morning for anyone from the club to be bothering him—especially since it was widely known that his office hours ended hours ago and he didn't like being disturbed unless it was an emergency. Or if it was the old man.

It couldn't possibly be the old man. Frank knew this because his father hadn't been much of a night owl for the last several years. And if his dad needed him at this hour, he'd most certainly use the cell.

Whoever was out there knocked again.

"C'mon in…"

The door yawned open.

Frank's jaw dropped. He stood up slowly from his chair.

Flanked by Torchia and Baines, the brunette stood in the doorway, her big blue eyes focused on him.

***

The big, broad-shouldered man looked totally perplexed.

He stood stiffly behind his desk, the muscles in his thick neck quivering the moment Julie walked into the room.

He was clean shaven and well dressed, at least six feet tall and well over two hundred pounds. He had thick, curly black hair and deep-set, angry black eyes. Julie figured him at around forty-five, maybe even fifty.

He was unquestionably the man she'd bumped into behind Schiller's six weeks earlier.

She could feel the vibes oozing from this man. They were strong as well as dark and cold. They told her he was frightened by her presence.

You can do this, child. He has no power over you.

Julie sensed that she had nothing to fear from this man.

She approached his desk and stopped a couple of feet from it. As she gazed at him, sensing the fear consuming him, she could tell that his spirit had taken refuge in some dark, cold place.

"You're the man who sent these two gentlemen to my place tonight," she said, gesturing to the two men standing behind her.

He said nothing. Instead, he shifted his gaze unsteadily toward her right, where one of the men would be standing. Without speaking, he gave a

217

very slight nod. About five seconds later, she heard the door quietly click shut behind her.

She could tell they were now alone in the room.

"Why'd you send them?" she asked.

Again, no reply.

"You might as well tell me. I don't intend to leave until you do."

With a tired groan, the man dropped into his chair, making it squeak. His eyes stayed on her as he brought the glass toward his face and nervously sipped from it. His hand continued shaking as he lowered the glass and placed it on the gray blotter in front of him.

Julie sighed. This was getting her nowhere. The sign on the door said this man, Frank Baroni, managed this club. Judging by the anger in his eyes, his large imposing size, and his arrogant appearance, he would have no problem instilling abject fear into his men or anyone else he encountered. This, however, did not intimidate her at all. Her inner voice had been right: this man had no power over her. But she still needed to clear this up. She also wanted to make sure he knew who he was dealing with.

"Was it something I did? Something I didn't do? Something I said? Something I didn't say?"

Silence. More darkness exuded from him.

"You can tell me. If you think I should be dead because of some stupid reason, I think I should know what we're talking about—don't you agree?"

Frank Baroni sat back in his chair. He seemed to relax a little. His gaze stayed on her. Julie could tell he was trying to evaluate the situation. She

218

could also sense some admiration emanating from him. He respected her for coming here to face him alone but hated her for having his men tag along, which made them look weak, helpless, and incompetent. It also made him out to be an ineffective boss.

Sorry about that, she thought, focusing.

A flicker of warm relief suddenly emanated from him.

It wasn't their fault, she added, fixed on his eyes. *They just didn't expect to encounter someone like me.*

A wave of frustration wafted over from him.

Sensing he was about to talk, she lowered herself into one of the two seats facing his desk. "I assume you're gonna try to drag this out, so I think I'd better make myself comfortable until you decide to tell me something that might make sense—"

"You got some heavy-duty 'nads, girl," he said flatly.

Apparently he'd found her last statement particularly irritating.

"I don't have those. In case you haven't noticed, I'm a woman."

"Believe me, I see that, but that don't mean you don't have a pair of gigantic stones…"

"I can be blunt when I have to be. And also when I don't want to waste time waiting for someone to answer—"

"Your name…it's Julie Kenner?"

"I'm sure you know that by now. And yours?"

His thick black brows jumped up. "You serious?"

She sensed that he was trying to get her to admit to something that might make him somehow regain his superiority. Though she clearly remembered the plate on the door, she didn't want him to think it made an impression. "If I knew, I wouldn't have asked."

He stared at her, his glare wavering. "I'm Frank Baroni. I own this place."

"Really?"

"Yeah. And you own that fancy little flower shop in Winter Park—"

"You know I do." It was her turn to bristle.

His thick black brows mashed together.

She could feel his aura lightening somewhat and decided to keep up the pressure. Not a lot, but just enough to make him realize she wasn't the type of person to be toyed with.

"Just a few days ago, an unpleasant little man badly needing a shower, a shave, some strong mouthwash, and clean clothes came to my place and invited me to walk outside with him and then step out into traffic."

He continued watching her in silence.

"Aren't you gonna ask me why he did that?"

He shrugged. "Now why would I ask you somethin' like that?"

"Probably because I think you most likely had something to do with his coming to see me."

"Why the hell would I want some stupid little bastard—"

"You *wanted* me to step out into traffic, didn't you?"

His nostrils flared.

"C'mon, now. You can do better than that…"

He took a deep breath. "Girl, I don't know what the hell you're talkin' about."

"You most certainly do."

"Now why the hell would I—"

"You want me dead. That's why that little guy came to my shop. That's also why one of those two men out there—" she jerked a thumb at the door behind her—"came to my shop just a day or two before that, and why those two snuck into my condo just an hour or so ago."

He opened his mouth to reply, but she was faster.

"Why on earth do you want me dead?"

No reply.

She sensed more fear filling up his spirit. An image from his thoughts blinked brightly for a moment before dimming. She could envision a heavyset bald man lying on the filthy ground near a dumpster at night, with an orange haze from an overhead lamp highlighting the man's face. A dark, circular-shaped pool had gathered on the ground beneath the man's head. A pair of glasses, both lenses broken, lay twisted on the ground about two feet from the man's left ear. The man was wearing a dark suit. His tan tie lay in a rumpled pile over his right shoulder.

Julie continued concentrating on Frank Baroni. Another image came up, this one just a few feet from the dead man, starting at his head and scanning the area toward his feet, where the lights of Schiller's Steakhouse lit up the building twenty or thirty yards down.

The solitary figure of a woman was walking toward the parking lot on the other side of the building.

Julie could tell by the outfit and the handbag that she was the woman. It happened the night she and Janie had dinner together after Julie had closed up the shop for the day.

But now she needed to know what was going on with this angry, nasty man.

"*Who is that woman?*" Julie asked the man mentally.

He didn't respond. His blank stare revealed nothing.

It is you, child...

Yes. I know.

The rest is up to you, now...

I know, but what can I do?

You'll know when the time is right.

"*I didn't see anything that night,*" she mentally told Frank Baroni.

A dark, blurry image of the two men taking her out into the woods filled his thoughts. The two men were the same two who had snuck into her condo. The same two who had brought her here.

"*I didn't see anything. I didn't hear anything, either.*"

An image of the two opening the trunk of the Charger and pulling out shovels showed clearly in his brain.

"I have no idea why you want me dead. I was leaving the restaurant that night, after my sister and I had dinner. I got in my car and drove away. Case closed."

222

He blinked as if pulling himself from a trance. He squinted at her and shook his head. Then he reached for his glass and drained it in one swallow. "I...don't know...what you're talkin' about, girl."

"You most certainly do."

He groaned. "Listen. I'm gonna tell you this one last time—"

"You're not gonna do *anything* to me from now on. Understand?"

"Girl—"

"Understand?"

Some inner sense suggested that he was much too stubborn and arrogant to listen to reason. This obviously required additional pressure, suggesting that she do something she wasn't familiar with. This made her wonder if she could do it.

You can do it, child...

But you don't know what I was thinking.

I know what I would do, under the same circumstances...

I just don't know if it would work for me.

Show me and I'll tell you...

Julie closed her eyes and focused.

Moments later, the inner voice said, *Very nice. It is much like what I would have done...*

Really?

I would never lie to you, child...

"Listen to me, girl." Frank Baroni sounded angry. "You can't prove that I've done or arranged anything, get it? You need proof. You need witnesses—"

"What about those two out in the hall?"

He sent over a loud, cruel chuckle. "You *really* think those two bozos'll be on *your* side? Especially if they know what'll happen to them if they—"

"Oh, I know perfectly well that they'll side with you."

The man grinned. "Okay, then."

"There's something *you* ought to know before you even think of doing anything else that involves me or my future."

He didn't reply, but she could tell he was interested.

"Before you arrange anything else that will hurt or do something even worse to anyone else, I want you to think of something first."

"Yeah? And what's that?"

She stared at him for a few moments, watching his eyes, which expressed both curiosity and fear.

"I'm still waitin'," he said with a loose shrug.

In a calm voice, she said, "Mistaking someone for someone else just might get you into a world of trouble."

Chapter 22

"Another drink?"

The shapely redhead walked over to Robert's table and smiled pleasantly.

He'd been here nearly half an hour and hadn't seen anyone familiar or heard anything out of the ordinary. The uncertainty of the situation had been making him more anxious than ever that Julie could be in serious trouble.

This made him even more determined to find her. He accepted the fact that she was a grown, independent woman who paid her own way and ran her own business. She was also very special, possessed an exceptional gift, and could probably hold her own with anyone. Hell, she'd done extraordinarily well on her own with the two thugs who had broken into her place, hadn't she?

Since he had no idea where to look or what to do, and was working completely on his own, he guessed that his best bet would be to find the office of the manager and work from there. Though he knew nothing about the man, he suspected that he could very well be the enemy, and might have even been directly involved in all this.

Robert didn't care. With Julie's safety in jeopardy, he wasn't concerned about who he had to deal with to find her. It was up to him to do whatever was necessary to make sure she was safe. And once he found her, he was determined to take her back to the safety of her condo.

He nodded to the waitress, who smiled and whisked away to get his refill. He didn't want her to get suspicious, so he decided to order another round. Once she returned, he'd pay for the drink, give her a generous tip, then leave and look for the office of the manager of the club.

***

Frank Baroni could feel the short black hairs bristling on the back of his neck.

This bitch had just threatened him. It was one thing to come to his office and talk smack to him, but quite another to threaten him.

"Mistaking someone for someone else just might get you into a world of trouble…"

What the hell was she talking about?

And just who *was* this bitch? She certainly was strange, the way she just waltzed right in here and started talking to him like she owned the damned place. She certainly had a giant set of 'nads for a babe. And the rest of her didn't exactly hurt her case. Great body, great legs, terrific hair…

Take those baby blues. The way they settled in on him made him feel like he was about to lose his lunch.

He hated to admit it, but Torchia was right, and so was that psycho Tripper. The way this female looked at you made you feel like pond scum for even thinking of doing anything to her. No wonder those two couldn't pull it off.

But there was no way in hell this bitch would pull the same shit with Frank Baroni!

He was the boss, dammit. Along with the old man, he was the most powerful club owner in the entire state. When Frank gave an order, it was carried out, no questions asked. When some dumbass got in his way, Frank made one phone call. One call and that was that. Once the call was made, one less dumbass was wandering around.

So why was this bitch sitting in his office, talking smack to him? Didn't she realize who she was dealing with?

And who the hell did she think she was, threatening him like that?

There was no way she could get away with this. There was one surefire way of letting her know who was running things, and she was about to get her first important lesson.

"What the hell are you talkin' about?"

She didn't reply. She just sat there, staring at him.

And staring.

Strange, all right. And creepy, as well.

But this didn't explain a damned thing. And it sure as hell didn't give her the right to threaten him or talk to him as if he was street scum. He knew right then that once he got rid of this bitch, he was gonna have it out with Torchia and Baines, and by the time he was finished with them, they wouldn't know which end was up.

"You know who you're talkin' to, don'tcha?"

Silence.

The staring continued.

What the hell was she pulling now?

"I just asked you a question. Didn't you hear me?"

"I heard you just fine."

His heart skipped a beat.

Was he imagining things? Or did she just say all that without moving her lips?

"*You're very tense, aren't you?*" she asked softly, again without moving her lips.

What the hell? How was she *doing* that?

"*I really think you should relax…and try to be calm…*"

"Listen here—"

"*Just relax and take a deep breath. You really should work on trying to calm yourself. You're all tense and wound up, aren't you?*"

"Look…"

He suddenly discovered that he was relaxing in the chair. He also realized that she was right, he *was* tense and wound up. But that was *her* fault. That was because…because…

He'd suddenly forgotten why he was so tense and wound up.

Then it came back. Sluggishly, but at least it had returned.

They were arguing, and this woman was getting to him. He still couldn't believe what she'd just said to him and was struggling to decide why she'd said it.

Why *had* she said it? Why had she just told him that…that what he had done…that he shouldn't…that…that…

What the hell?

He suddenly realized that he'd forgotten why they were arguing in the first place. He knew it had something to do with why he was so tense, but he just couldn't quite wrap his head around the

228

conversation. He tried, but nothing would come. He tried again, but after that second failure, decided he no longer cared. He'd grown quite comfortable in his chair and found that he thoroughly enjoyed the sensation, Hell with everything else, he was just gonna sit here in this comfortable chair, and if anyone didn't like it, they could just go screw themselves and…and…

His eyelids were becoming heavy.

The room gradually grew dimmer.

His temper softened, and suddenly it was gone, and he began wondering once again why he'd been so angry, so stressed…

Before he realized it, his chair had grown softer…

Frank discovered that he felt even more relaxed than just moments ago.

His eyes remained closed, and he soon found that he was peacefully nestled in a quiet world of soft warmth.

Just as things grew darker, he had the strange sensation that someone with big blue eyes was watching him…

Then he heard a soft, soothing voice whispering things to him… Things he could not quite understand…

The voice eventually grew softer and softer, until he no longer heard it.

The blue eyes gradually dimmed…

Then…blackness…

***

Bill Torchia cringed when he saw the brunette's boyfriend walking down the hall in their direction.

Jocko Baines had been leaning against the wall just a few feet from the office door when the man appeared around the corner. Baines immediately straightened and moved closer to where Bill was standing. "What the fuck's *he* doin' here?" Baines whispered.

Icy fear crept down Bill's spine, and he shivered. "He must've followed us."

Baines groaned. "He can't be here, goddammit. The boss sees him, he'll freak, and we can kiss our asses bye-bye!"

"I hear you." Bill knew full well that something very bad would happen if the boyfriend pressed the issue and demanded to see Frank. If Bill was right about the guy, he wouldn't leave or cooperate unless he was convinced the girl was all right. Bill didn't know the man but had seen definite signs of bravado and could recognize a capable adversary when he saw one. The man was true-blue and would go all the way to protect his woman. He hadn't been reluctant at all about positioning himself in front of her to shield her from Baines' gun. Not too many would have done that same thing. It made Bill wonder if the guy had had military training.

True-blue, all right. A rarity these days.

But that didn't tell him how they were going to handle this.

"*You* wanna take care of this?" Baines' right hand had instinctively moved toward the Sig in his waistband. "Or ya want *me* to do it?"

Something like this could not happen—not here, anyway. If any violence or bloodshed happened outside Frank's office, there would be

230

hell to pay. Frank hated negative publicity and would make sure both Bill and Jocko would pay the price if any whisper of scandal or murder investigation developed to put the club in the spotlight.

"I'll take it. And be careful with that thing. This isn't exactly the best place to use it."

"I still got the silencer."

"You actually think a *silencer* will take care of this?"

"Can't hurt." Baines shrugged loosely.

Bill shook his head. Baines could be *such* a moron. "*You* want to tell the cops about the bloodstains messing up the carpet? How about blood spatter on the wallpaper?"

Jocko groaned and let his hand drop to his side.

Bill nervously walked up to the guy. "You know you're not supposed to be back here, don'tcha?" he asked amicably.

The other man appeared both frightened and angry. "I could figure that out on my own, thanks."

"Then let me save you some aggravation by guiding you back down the hall—"

"You know damned well why I'm here and why I'm not interested at all in you or anyone else guiding me back down the hall. The best thing you can do right now is to make this as painless as possible for all of us by telling me where my girlfriend is."

Bill knew all about the frightened/angry combo. He'd seen its devastating effect too many times in Iraq. Being both frightened and angry frequently caused panic, desperation, and a slew of other negative reactions as well. While very few examples resulted in victory or heroic action, most others caused death, injury, chaos, and other equally disgusting outcomes. Bill decided that since this man was going to be stubborn, a little vagueness might just work. "Now why would you think your girlfriend would—"

"Please don't underestimate me." The man's anger had quickly taken over. "If you'd like to know if I have actual working brain matter in my head, let me give you a capsulized example. I run my own business. I can also dress myself and make my own bed. In other words, I'm fully functional."

"I didn't realize I was—"

"You're assuming I'm either stupid or ignorant. I'm telling you right here and now that I'm neither, and if you keep thinking I am—"

"I'm only trying to say—"

"In case you think I might not know what's going on, here's what I've got so far. You and your friend, here, broke into Julie's condo. Your friend pointed a gun at us. After talking to her, you put her in your car, brought her here, and drove to the back of the building, which leads to the rear EXIT. I may not be familiar with this place, but I'd venture a guess and say that same door goes to the rear steps, which leads to this hall. Let me know how I'm doing so far."

So much for the vagueness…

"Listen." Bill lowered his voice. He glanced at Baines, who was standing just six feet or so behind the boyfriend, his hand nervously tapping his right thigh. "Your girlfriend is fine. She's—"

"Where *is* she?"

"I said she's fine. She's talking to the manager of the club, and—"

"I don't believe you."

Bill sighed. This was tougher than he'd guessed. But he should have figured that it wouldn't be easy. If this same girl had been Bill's girlfriend, he'd not only be just as suspicious as this guy, but he'd probably be tearing the club apart by now, piece by piece, looking for her.

But that wasn't the issue. He had to do something to keep a lid on this, and he had to do it quickly.

"You have to believe me. When I said—"

"Why should I believe anything you say? You broke into her place and threatened both of us—"

"I realize that, and I'm sorry."

"Uh-huh…"

"I really am. And believe me, if I were in your shoes—"

"Well, you're not, but I am, and I intend to find out where she is and who she's with. I don't care how big and tough you and your friend are, this girl means the world to me, and I intend to find her. And when I do, she'd better be in the same condition she was when she left the condo. Otherwise, I intend to go after both of you, your boss, and probably his boss as well. I'm sure you realize what this type of situation will do to the future of this club."

Bill realized right then that he had this guy pegged right all along. Besides being a true-blue, standup guy, he was going up against Bill, Baines, Frank, and Carlo as well. The man was dead serious and clearly meant every word he'd said. He admired the man. He sincerely hoped he didn't have to hurt him.

"What's your name?" Bill asked.

"Why?"

"I like to know the name of the man I'm talking to."

"I'm Robert Townsend."

"Tell you what, Robert," Bill said. "If you wait another fifteen minutes, I promise you we'll—"

"Why would I want to do that?"

"'Cause we *said* so." Baines had decided he'd heard enough. He moved a step closer to Townsend. "And when we say so—"

"You're not scaring me," Townsend said.

"We don't want to *scare* you," Bill said. "We just want you to know—"

"I don't care if you're fuckin' scared or what." Baines's voice had already grown louder. "We tell ya to wait fifteen minutes, we mean ya wait fifteen minutes. Got it? Or do I gotta knock ya on your ass and make sure ya lie there like a good boy for fifteen fuckin' minutes?"

The man almost smiled. He turned to Bill. "Your friend's a real piece of work, isn't he?"

Bill forced himself to hold in a good laugh.

Baines snorted and moved even closer. His face was mere inches from Townsend's. "You *tryin'* to piss me off, asshole?" At that same moment, his right hand twitched.

"I'm not *trying* to do *any*thing. I just gave your friend a straightforward observation. If you can't handle the truth, that's *your* problem, isn't it?"

Baines blinked. His forehead filled with lines. "Huh?"

Townsend turned to Bill. "Not very bright, is he?"

Bill's pulse quickened when he saw Baines' hand moving closer to the Sig. "Listen, Robert...if I were you, I wouldn't—"

"As I said before, you're not me. And if this idiot's going for his gun and intends to use it right here, he really *is* mental. I mean batshit crazy. A loony bird. Just a step or two from the rubber room."

Baines had had it. He moved close enough to Townsend to reach out and strangle the man. "All right, asshole. You're askin' for it!"

Bill stepped in between them and watched in utter terror as Jocko's right hand disappeared underneath his shirt.

Chapter 23

"I'm very glad we finally had our nice little talk," a strange woman's voice said.

Frank Baroni's eyes shot open.

Startled, he glanced about the room.

His office. Why, of course it was. He was sitting at his desk, as always. His bottle of Scotch stood on the desk just a foot away from his right elbow. Next to it, his glass, with just a swallow or two left in it. The bottle was way less than half full. He couldn't remember when he'd opened it.

He also couldn't remember what time of day it was.

Had he zoned out? Seriously? In his office?

He rubbed his eyes. When his vision cleared, he noticed movement straight ahead.

A slender brunette was heading for the door.

What the hell was going on? Who the hell was that babe?

What was she doing in here?

Was this some sort of business meeting?

Why the hell couldn't he remember?

"What are you doin' in here?" he asked loudly, trying to reclaim control of the situation.

Before she reached the door, she turned, smiled brightly, and waved. She had the most incredible blue eyes. He couldn't help wondering if she was one of the club dancers. He couldn't remember. It didn't help one bit that most of the babes working there had similar facial features.

Although his head remained cloudy, he struggled to recall every dancer working in the place. How many were there? Twelve? Fifteen? Or were there more?

And what about the waitresses? Four on each shift, and every one of them hot enough to work the damn pole.

He needed to get a better look.

"Hey! Girl!"

"Bye, now."

"We need to talk!"

"We already did."

"When?"

"Just a minute or so ago."

What the hell did she mean by *that*?

Why couldn't he remember?

Wouldn't he remember talking to a babe looking like her? A babe with those eyes?

Wouldn't *any* guy with the usual urges remember a babe who looked like her?

"I can't remember a damned—"

"You will. Just sit there for a few moments. It'll come to you." She smiled at him and he suddenly felt less tense than just moments ago. Those gorgeous blue eyes seemed to have a tremendous effect on him.

While he sat back and began to chill, the woman pulled open the door, walked out into the hall, and closed the door quietly behind her.

He wanted to jump up and run after her, but something prevented him from doing so. He seemed so comfortable in his chair that he didn't want to get out of it. So instead of jumping up and running over to the door, he chose to remain in his chair, staring at the closed door while trying to figure out what had just transpired in his office. He vaguely recalled Torchia and Baines bringing someone with them when they came in.

Was it this chick? Or someone else?

Why did everything seem like it happened a long time ago?

Was it *that* long ago? Or just a few minutes? If so, wouldn't he remember? And why had he zoned out?

He *did* zone out, didn't he? What else would you call this?

A babe leaves this office, and for some stupid reason I can't begin to figure out, I can't even remember who she was or why she was here!

It didn't matter, did it? What mattered was who they'd brought in. It had to have been that woman, right? The one he wanted dead?

But why had they brought her *here*?

Did it have anything to do with that nasty Morgan Betz business?

No. That babe was different. The one who'd just left his office was definitely not her. Different hair, different face. Different body. She didn't even move in the same manner.

But if she wasn't that chick, who the hell *was* she?

He sat very still, his head down, his eyes closed, struggling to recall the last few minutes. It took him just a little while before he realized Torchia and Baines must have brought in that woman.

But why?

He closed his eyes even tighter and struggled to concentrate. Moments later, his thoughts cleared, and he guessed that the brunette who had just left his office was indeed the woman those two had brought in, although she wasn't the one he'd wanted them to deal with.

She really *was* a different chick, wasn't she?

Of *course* she was.

Wasn't she?

Once again, he struggled to recall every detail about the woman he'd bumped into behind Schiller's. *Was* it the same girl? Or was she someone else entirely?

What was different about this one?

The face, of course. The hair was the same, but the face was a different shape, and the eyes seemed, well, totally wrong.

Was it the same chick?

Of *course* it was. It *had* to be. Who else *could* it have been?

Just when he thought he had the answer, the doubt came right back and whacked him in the face. The girl leaving his office was *not* the girl he wanted out of the way. The one behind the restaurant, the one who'd seen him walking away after icing Betz, was the same height and weight, the same body shape, and...

They were different women. Totally different.

The most important question of all hit him, making him realize how confused he really was.

Even if that chick *was* the same girl they'd brought in, it didn't explain what was bothering him most of all.

What the hell was she doing in here with me?

***

Julie opened the office door and cringed.

Robert was standing out in the hall with the two bouncers.

"Robert?" She couldn't believe he'd come here—especially since she'd told him to stay in the condo. "Wh-What are you *doing* here?"

Robert spun around. The men facing him had stiffened the moment they saw her. Neither said anything.

"You're...okay?" Robert asked, surprised.

"I'm fine."

"You're sure?"

She didn't know how she should feel right now. Should she be angry with him? Thrilled that he'd cared enough about her to follow them to the club? Should she feel honored? Worried? Terrified? Or upset that he'd totally disregarded what she'd told him and followed them here?

She was extremely glad that he was okay. She could feel genuine rage coming from the bigger of the two—the one who'd held them at gunpoint in her condo. She could tell that he wanted to do something horrible to Robert.

She felt very relieved that she'd shown herself before something terrible happened.

What was next on the agenda?

After all, she'd just used mind control on their boss. It would be only a minute or so before he

240

recovered. Once this happened, he'd want to find out who she was and where she'd gone.

It was extremely vital that she and Robert got out of here.

"I'm fine," she told him.

"What happened in there?" He glanced at the door.

"Later." She grasped his hand. "C'mon." She gave him a tug. "We need to leave."

"Our boss. He just let you *go*?" The good-looking one glanced at the office door, then at them again.

"I just left."

"Just like that?"

She shrugged. "We had our little talk. Then I told him I had to get back home."

"He was okay with that?" He sounded skeptical.

"He did ask me why you brought me here..."

The man swallowed loudly. "And what...what did you tell him?"

Julie could clearly see fear in the man's eyes.

"Well, I told him I wanted to see him—"

"And?"

"He asked me why, so I told him that I had a talk with you and your friend, and we all decided that I needed to talk with him to clear this all up."

"Cl-Clear this all up?" The man's voice was unsteady.

"After a while, we both decided that this was all just one big misunderstanding."

The man's dark eyes grew.

"He said he must've had me confused with someone else."

The man didn't reply.

"Don't sound like him," the other guy said, frowning.

"That's what he said…"

Neither men said anything.

"It was okay, believe me." Julie glanced at the door. So far, so good. But they were running out of time.

Use your gift, child…

She focused on both men. "You won't mind if we just left, will you?"

No response.

"We really do have to go." She smiled brightly at them.

Silence.

"It was terribly nice of you to bring me here and clear this up with your boss."

"Then he was…okay…with this?" The good-looking one sounded completely baffled.

"He let me leave, didn't he?"

Both men gawked at one another.

This is so nice of you to let us leave, she thought, focusing. *I'm sorry you're both gonna be so confused when you try to remember me. I wish this didn't have to happen, but I've really got no choice…*

She nudged Robert. "Let's go," she whispered.

"But—"

"*Now*, Robert."

He was about to say something, but she looked deeply into his eyes and said very softly, "We need to be gone. Right now."

Without another word, he grasped her hand tightly and led her briskly down the hall.

***

"Where the fuck is that brunette?"

Frank Baroni bulled his way out into the hall. All he saw were the two oversized idiots standing beside one another, looking clueless. There was no sign of the brunette, and this angered him even more than the two morons gawking at him so stupidly.

Torchia swallowed. "She, uh, left, Boss..."

"She *left*?"

A nod.

"Who the fuck *was* she?"

Both glanced at one another and shrugged.

Frank desperately wanted to knock a couple of heads together and decided that the two idiots standing just two feet away were the most deserving candidates. The fact that they were so close by made the impulse even more appealing.

But then he realized how detrimental that would be. He had his blood pressure to consider. It wouldn't be very bright for him to do something that could land him in Intensive Care.

He took a few breaths to calm down. "Any idea what she was doin' in my office?"

"We really don't know, Boss," Torchia stammered softly. "She made us bring her here. She said she wanted to talk to you."

"She *made* you bring her here?"

243

A nod from Torchia.

This sounded ridiculous.

"How much do you two bozos tip the scales?"

They both looked as if he had just asked them something in a different language.

"Your weight, dammit. How much do you two weigh?"

Torchia frowned. "Two-twenty, Boss…"

"And you, Baines?"

"Two-forty-eight…"

"How much do ya think that girl goes? One-fifteen? One-twenty, maybe?"

No response.

"She hold a gun on you?"

"A gun, Boss?" from Torchia.

"A gun, you idiot. Like the one Baines carries in his waistband. I'm sure the two of you have seen a couple of 'em before—especially you, Torchia, since you were in the damn military. A gun. It's got a butt, a barrel, and bullets. The bullets are loud and make giant, bloody holes in people. In other words, bang, bang, and somebody's dead. Did she have one of those?"

"No, Boss…"

"But you said she *made* you drive her here?"

Torchia nodded. Baines merely shrugged a massive shoulder and continued looking stupid.

"Either of you two wanna tell me how she did that?"

Baines didn't speak.

Torchia said, "She told us to bring her here."

Frank wanted to knock their heads together just to see if any actual brain matter squirted out of their

244

ears and spilled on the carpet. "Okay, then... She doesn't have a gun and weighs about as much as one of your legs. Despite all that, she told you to bring her here. Is that about it?"

Torchia nodded.

"She say *why* she wanted to talk to me?"

No response.

"You don't know? Neither of you?"

Silence.

"You brought a female to my office and you don't even know *why*?"

More silence.

Frank rubbed his temples and tried once again to recall what had happened. Had he had some sort of memory lapse? Had he fainted? His last doctor's exam revealed high blood pressure, but nothing to worry about. Shit like that came with the territory when you owned and operated a club and had to deal with pampered babes, the liquor license board, corrupt politicians, the local mob, tax laws, and horny guys. And, of course, idiots like these two. No big shakes, right? He'd been doing this shtick for years and had been doing it quite well.

But it didn't explain what that woman was doing in his office, and it sure as hell didn't tell him why he couldn't remember what had gone on between the two of them.

But now she was gone, and the only bodies out there were Torchia and Baines, who looked like posterchildren for dumb and dumber. And when they turned to each other with totally ignorant expressions, Frank knew he wasn't getting anything out of these two clowns but bullshit and more obvious signs of stupid.

"In my office," he barked. "*Now*!"

***

Using the rear EXIT, Julie and Robert made it outside without incident.

Due to the late hour, the front lot was less than half-filled. The only signs of life at the front entrance were the two bouncers. One looked bored as he played with his wristwatch while the other watched the traffic zipping down the Trail just beyond the front entrance of the club.

"What the hell happened in there?" Robert asked as they hurried over to the BMW.

Julie eyed the front of the building but saw nothing they should be concerned about. Then she glanced at the northern end of the building to make sure no one was coming for them from that direction. She saw nothing suspicious but didn't want to tempt fate. Even though she believed in her gift and its strange powers, she didn't want to take a chance. Not with Robert standing in the crosshairs with her.

And she still wasn't one hundred percent certain that what she'd done to Frank Baroni—or his two bouncers—was as effective as she hoped. She couldn't fully comprehend or accept what had happened during the last half-hour, but it was painfully obvious that now was not the right time or place to analyze things. The fact that she'd been able to survive a very tense, unpleasant encounter with a powerful man who wanted her dead was more than enough to process for now.

However, she suspected that they still weren't out of the woods.

"We need to get out of here. We can talk on the way back to my place."

As soon as they both got in the BMW, Robert fired up the ignition, pulled out of the space, and hurried over to the front entrance.

"By the way, why'd you follow us?" She could no longer stand the suspense.

"Why do you think?"

She really wanted to be angry at him but knew that would be impossible as well as ridiculous. He'd risked his own personal safety for her.

Twice, in fact.

At the condo, he'd positioned himself directly in front of her to protect her from possible gunfire. She didn't want to say anything about it at the time for fear of angering the thug holding the gun. The second instance occurred just a few minutes ago, when he'd faced the same two out in the hall. She knew the good-looking one wouldn't have bullied him too much. The vibes coming from him had told her he'd been forced to do some terrible things he desperately wanted to forget. Deep down, he was a genuinely nice guy and would hurt someone only if it was necessary.

However, the dark, foul vibes emanating from the other guy told her that he'd used his gun before and liked it. She also sensed that he enjoyed hurting people. He was very angry and would have done something terrible to Robert if she hadn't come out of the manager's office when she did.

Robert had not only gone there to find her but had also stood up to them. For her, and for what they had. This made her realize just how much she loved this man and how much she appreciated having him in her life.

"Give up?" he asked, still waiting for her reply.

"I think I might have *some* idea…"

"Go ahead, give it a shot. Maybe you'll get lucky."

"I want you to take me back to the condo right now." She rested her hand on his thigh.

"That's funny. I was thinking the very same thing."

Chapter 24

"We'll start right from the beginning, and let's do it right this time, okay?"

Frank Baroni was desperate to find out what was going on. None of this had made any sense, and it was bothering him. He didn't even care if it took the rest of the night to get to the truth.

"I wanna hear every goddamn detail," he added sourly.

Neither Torchia nor Baines spoke, but Torchia gave a slight nod, suggesting that they were at least paying attention.

Frank realized that it wasn't all their fault. As much as he wanted to blame them for whatever was going on, he knew he couldn't.

He couldn't, simply because he wasn't able to understand any of it himself.

The first thing he couldn't understand was that he'd actually nodded off in his office with someone else there, then woke up just as his visitor—an incredibly hot, good-looking babe—was leaving. And every single time he thought about this, he discovered that he didn't have any idea what she was doing here in the first place.

This was enough to scare the living shit out of anyone—especially Frank, who had never had any trouble whatsoever remembering anything. And the simple fact that this involved a beautiful woman made this mystery even more frustrating.

"You two brought her into my office—is this accurate?"

Torchia said, "Yes, sir."

Baines nodded.

"You brought her here because she *told* you to bring her here?"

"Yes, Boss," from Torchia.

"You brought her here because she wanted to talk to me."

Both nodded.

"But she didn't say what she wanted to talk to me about."

"No, Boss," Torchia said.

"All right. At least we got *that* figured out. So…you brought her here into my office. I don't expect you to tell me anything else because you two weren't in here with her."

"No, Boss."

"Both of you were out there in the hall, lookin' stupid—right?"

Torchia didn't reply, but Baines nodded.

"What *can* you tell me?"

Torchia shrugged. "Do you want to know what happened when she came out of your office, Boss?"

Frank groaned. "That would be a real humdinger of a place to start…"

"When she came out, I wondered what was going on, so I asked her, and she said you just let you go."

"*That's* what she said?"

Baines cleared his throat awkwardly. "Boss, she said she just left."

"Just like that?"

Torchia said, "What she said was, "We had our little talk and I told him I had to get back home.""

250

"And then?"

"She left."

"I *know* she left, moron. I went out there to flag her down, but all I saw were you two, and neither of you look like her. That would be what you'd call a red flag, wouldn't it?"

Silence.

"She left with a guy," Baines mumbled.

"She *what*?"

"A guy came and got 'er," Baines replied.

"Whaddya mean, a guy came and got her?"

"A guy came lookin' for her, Boss."

Frank felt his blood pressure spiking again. He took a breath. "Go on..."

"He's her boyfriend," Torchia said.

"And he was out there with you? Out there? In the hall?"

Both nodded.

Great. Just fucking great. "And he showed up right outside my office door?"

"He followed us here," Torchia said. "From the woman's condo."

Frank took another deep breath. "He was with the girl when you found her?"

Torchia nodded.

"Why the fuck didn't ya tell me about this before now?"

"It didn't come up yet," Torchia said.

"All right. This woman's boyfriend came and got her. What happened after that?"

"They left," Torchia replied.

"Just like that?"

They both nodded.

Frank cringed at the sudden nausea. It dawned on him that this could turn very bad. If the boyfriend wanted to press charges, he could nail Torchia and Baines for kidnapping, trespassing, unlawful detainment, physical assault—

Too many damned things—especially if Torchia or Baines—or both of them—decided to bring Frank into this. Then the old man would—

No. No sense in even worrying about this. At least not yet, anyway.

Frank took a deep breath and rubbed his temples. "Tell me about this boyfriend."

Torchia shrugged. "He followed us here, Boss. Once he found her, he left with her. That was about it."

"You sure?"

"All he wanted was to find her. He was worried."

"Think he'll cause problems?"

"Ya mean for the club, Boss? Baines asked.

Frank sighed and shook his head. It was a damned shame that a muscular monster like Baines had to be such an idiot. "No. I meant, do you think this asshole will run for public office. *Of course* I meant for the club, you moron!"

"All he cared about was finding her and taking her back to her place," Torchia said. "I don't think he'll sue you or the club—if that's what you mean…"

"That's exactly what I mean. But how do you know for sure?"

"We don't. Not for sure, anyway. But he didn't strike me as a lawsuit-minded kind of guy."

"Didn't get that vibe from him?"

Torchia shook his head. "He's a standup kinda guy. Honest. Respectful. All he cared about was getting her back and if she was okay. Once he saw that she was okay and hadn't been hurt or traumatized, he seemed satisfied."

"What if you're wrong?"

"We'll stand up for you, Boss."

Baines nodded.

Frank grabbed the bottle of Scotch and poured some into his glass. While the two continued standing nervously behind the two chairs facing the desk, he drained the glass and then sat back in his chair. The Scotch made him feel slightly better, so he decided to be less harsh. Sighing tiredly, he gestured for them to sit.

As they carefully circled the chairs, he said, "Let's get back to the most important issue, then. Did the girl say anything else?"

The two glanced at one another. Frank could tell they were afraid to say anything.

"I'm waitin'…"

Torchia was obviously holding something back.

"Did you let her go because of the boyfriend? Because you were afraid he'd make a stink? Or is there something else you haven't said?"

Torchia shrugged. "Boss, she's got this way about her…"

"What the fuck are ya talkin' about now?"

Torchia shook his head. "She's got this way…of…of looking at a guy—"

"Now what the fuck does *that* have to do with anything?"

253

Torchia shrugged. "It confuses a guy."

"Huh?"

"The way she looks at you. It confuses you, and you forget what you're gonna say."

Frank suddenly remembered something that had happened to him right here, in this office. It was something that caused a tiny flicker in his head. The moment he tried remembering, he realized that he was looking for something that was no longer in his head. He had a feeling it was important and that it involved the woman...but he just couldn't pin it down. The moment this happened, it dawned on him that what Torchia had just said made him realize what must have happened.

"Both of you are dead certain that she didn't say why she wanted you to bring her here?"

Baines was the one who spoke up this time. He sounded somewhat dazed. "She just said she *wanted* us to, Boss..."

"She *wanted* you to bring her here? Nothing else?"

Both men nodded.

He watched both men until a fresh idea suddenly developed in his head. It was something he'd never considered before, and it convinced him right off that it was extremely important, and that he'd been very foolish for not thinking about it before now. "Describe this girl."

"Boss?"

"Just do it."

"You mean, what she looked like?" Baines asked.

Frank felt the urge to knock their heads together coming back. "You don't think I care about the woman's *mind*, do ya? Or her opinion about how she thinks about plunging necklines?"

Baines shrugged. "No, Boss…"

"I'm *so* glad you're finally on top of things. Yeah. Let's go with what she looks like, for now. Describe her."

Torchia said, "I'd guess around five-eight, slender, long legged, exceptionally good-looking—"

"Describe her face."

"Extremely good-looking, as I just said."

"I know what you said. Now describe her features."

"All I can remember is that she had the most incredible blue eyes."

At least they agreed on that. But even so, that wasn't quite enough, and he knew he had to dig deeper. "Nothin' else?"

Torchia scratched the back of his thick neck.

"How about hair?"

Torchia shrugged. "Reddish brown. More red than brown, I'd say."

"Looked dark brown to me," Baines said. "And I don't think she was five-eight."

"How tall would you say she was?"

"Five-ten. Maybe five-eleven. A tall babe."

"She was wearing two-inch heels," Torchia said.

"They looked more like spikes," Baines said. "That made her only about an inch or two shorter than me."

255

"Funny," Torchia said, turning to Baines. "To me, she seemed at least three inches shorter than me, and you're an inch taller than I am."

"Maybe she wasn't five-ten at all," Baines said. "Maybe she *was* five-eight."

Torchia suddenly looked confused. "Now I think she might have been five-six…or seven."

"Forget her damn height." Frank was getting irritated again. "How 'bout her bust size?"

"Average," from Torchia.

Baines grinned devilishly. "Nice ones. Nice, *nice* size."

Frank rubbed the back of his neck. It was obvious something very strange was going on. He just didn't know what the hell it was or how to deal with it. The woman they were talking about was a looker, but these two couldn't even describe her. Frank, however, didn't think that was odd because he couldn't remember what the girl looked like, either. In his memory, she had long, medium brown hair. Not reddish brown, and certainly not more red than brown.

But when she'd turned around and smiled at him before leaving the office, all he could remember were those big blue eyes.

And when he tried to remember the face of the woman he'd bumped into at Schiller's Steakhouse, he imagined one of the pole dancers. Not the woman who had just left his office, but one of the damn *pole dancers*.

Had he been wrong about this all along?

Had something gone totally haywire in his brain?

With a shaky hand, he splashed more Scotch into his glass and sucked it right down. Once the fire ebbed in his gut, he gazed at the two men facing him. "Was there anything else this woman said to you in the hall before I came out?"

Torchia didn't reply.

Baines nodded.

"I'm listenin'…"

"She said she was sorry we were so confused about everything, Boss," Baines said softly.

Frank turned to Torchia. "That sound right to you?"

Torchia swallowed audibly. "I-I'm n-not sure, Boss…"

"What do you think she said, then?"

Torchia didn't reply. He began studying the floor again.

Chapter 25

"Are you *sure* we don't have to worry about anyone else coming after us?"

Julie could tell Robert was still unnerved by what had happened at BABES APLENTY. She was determined to dispel his fears and knew she was going to have to be very careful about how she did it.

Even so, she couldn't help feeling genuine relief as she brought over two small pieces of vanilla cheesecake. Her relief had nothing to do with what she had done at the strip club; it was just a feeling she had. She handed him one of the plates and sat down at the kitchen table. "Positive."

"How can you be so sure?"

She took a sip of bourbon and shrugged. "It's very simple. He won't remember me."

His brows pushed together. "A girl who looks like you? Seriously?"

"You don't *want* him to, do you?"

"Well, no…"

"Okay, then." She picked up her fork.

"What about those other two? You know, the classy duo that wanted to pick me up and toss me through the nearest window?"

"They won't remember, either."

He stared at her the longest time before responding. "Care to explain that one to me? I mean, it's not like you've got a forgettable face, you know. In my book, you're just as classy as any of

258

those dancers I saw at that club. The waitresses, too."

"Thank you, but that's not exactly what we're talking about."

"All right. Now, I guess, would be a good time to clear this up. I seem to be getting this strange notion that you did some sort of hypnosis to the owner, as well as two of his employees."

"Hypnosis?" She hadn't expected him to pick up on this so easily.

"I've been thinking about this special gift you told me about. I'm trying to figure out exactly what it is but, to be honest, I'm not having much luck."

"What do you think it is?"

"From what you've told me, I'd say it's much more than my little mind can comprehend. From what I've already gathered, your gift has saved my life and also the life of a very astonished cab driver. It has also done a number, as you've already said, to the owner of this club, who wanted you dead, and his two employees, who watched us leave the place and did nothing to stop us. I'm sure you must know that, under normal circumstances, they would have most likely detained us while they asked their boss if it was okay for us to leave. But now you're telling me that he no longer wants you dead because he simply won't remember you. How am I doing so far?"

She didn't want to tell him that she'd made a tiny suggestion to Frank Baroni's mind that would literally scramble his memory whenever he tried putting together what had happened behind Schiller's that night he'd murdered that poor man.

Her suggestion would become a permanent voice in his head and would automatically substitute faces from the man's past to create a sort of montage that would interfere with his thought processes. She didn't want to tell Robert any of this because she didn't understand the true power of her gift and also because it scared her to think she possessed the ability to manipulate someone mentally.

Her reasoning was simple. What she had with Robert was very real. It was very real and very wonderful, and she refused to do anything that would threaten it even in the tiniest way.

"That's about it," she told Robert, and hoped he believed her.

"Are you sure?" He sounded doubtful.

"I can't tell you much more..."

"Why not?"

"Because I honestly don't fully understand any of it myself."

"Then tell me what you *do* understand."

Just then, the soft, wonderful inner voice returned.

Tell him what you know, child.

"I don't think I can," she told the voice.

I think you can.

"But I'm just not sure about what any of this is."

Tell him what you are *sure about, then...*

The only thing she could fully understand was that she could sense someone's moods and thoughts, and that she sometimes felt she could influence what someone was thinking...or feeling.

What else, child?

260

"I can influence someone's thoughts, can't I?"

To a degree.

"How much of a degree?"

As much as you need to make sure no one gets hurt.

"Even if it means getting into someone's brain and making them change their mind about something?"

As long as it spares someone's life. Our gift is that of love, child. Always remember that. And never forget that little bit of sunshine you shall always hold in the palm of your hand.

"I guess it's like being nice to someone when you want them to change their mind about doing something bad," she finally said.

"That's *all* it is?" He still sounded doubtful.

"Basically."

"Even though you manage to do it a little differently?"

Once again she was afraid he'd caught on a little too easily.

"What do you mean, differently?"

"To put it simply, from the inside out."

"What?"

"You go in through the mind."

She couldn't help smiling. "You're saying I can read minds even though I told you I can't?"

"How else could you influence someone the way you did back at the club?"

"As I've told you, I sense feelings and emotions. If I sense a negative one, I simply try to change it."

"Just like that?"

261

She shrugged. "Sometimes it works."

"It's been working pretty well since I've met you."

"I guess I've always been lucky."

He sighed tiredly and picked up his glass.

"You're not doubting me, are you?"

"Now why should I want to do a stupid thing like that?"

She smiled. "I don't know. Maybe because you are?"

"What? Stupid?"

She frowned. "Doubting me, silly."

"Sorry, but I just can't help it."

"Why not?"

"You sense things and know they're gonna happen before they do. Why should I think you can't read minds as well? Judging by the number of times you've picked *my* brain in the last couple of days, I've got to challenge you on that one."

"I can't, Robert. Honestly." She shook her head.

"You're not lying to me, are you?"

"Why would I want to do *that*?"

"Maybe because you don't want me to be afraid of you."

"Well? Are you?"

"Not *afraid*…"

"What, then?"

"Let's just say I know that if I press the issue, you just might decide to show me exactly what you *really* can do."

"You think I'd actually do something like that to you?"

He didn't reply. She could sense some embarrassment.

"Don't want to say?"

He just smiled sheepishly.

"How about if I promise you I'd never do something like that?"

"And how do you intend to do that?"

"By telling you I won't?"

"All right, then. Tell me."

"Actually, I'd rather show you."

"How are you gonna do that?"

"By doing it in another room."

"How will that convince me?"

"Let's call that the room where we never lie to one another."

"I didn't know such a room actually exists."

"I just said it did."

He smiled, and she could sense his relief. "I think I can live with that."

Chapter 26

Frank Baroni spent the late morning in his den, struggling once again to comprehend what had happened in his office eight hours earlier.

The harder he thought about it, the more complex everything seemed.

Once the confusion and the frustration became unbearable, he sat back in his seat and closed his eyes. He hoped that by doing so, he might be able to instill a sense of calm within himself, which might help to clear things up.

He remained in this state for several minutes, until he realized that the answer he was seeking was simply not there. He had to face the cold, harsh reality that a woman had seen him murder someone, a woman whose face he simply could not remember. For a while he thought he had, but something strange had recently affected his memory, preventing him from visualizing both the woman and the events as they'd happened. And as a direct result of this sudden unexplained mental decline, he'd come very close to having an innocent woman killed.

Angry with himself and with things in general, he struggled yet again to bring back the nightmare.

Once again, he found that, despite his efforts, the image just would not come. Everything else seemed to be there, and with great clarity. The body of Morgan Betz lying near the dumpster. The alley. The rear lot of Schiller's Steakhouse. Even the streetlight illuminating Colonial Drive…

But nothing else.

Each time the slim figure of a young woman with long legs and long, dark hair flashed in his brain, he discovered that she had no face. At one point, he thought the image had come to him, but the moment he focused on it, he found that the face strongly resembled his wife. When he tried once again concentrating on it just fifteen minutes later, the same phenomenon happened again. This time, however, the picture showing in his head had morphed into the face of a lap dancer who had left the club a year or so ago after meeting and marrying a bank president.

He thought it frightening to accept the harsh reality of how unstable the human mind could be. He found it even more terrifying that this was happening to him now, at just forty-six years of age, reminding him that, through no fault of his own, he had inherited memory loss from his grandfather, who died from Alzheimer's at sixty.

His cell went off. It was Tony Marciano, his day manager, calling on Facetime.

"What's goin' on?"

"Got a hopeful here for ya, Boss." Tony looked excited. "Sassy and hot, and she's only twenty-two. The books say she danced for close to eleven months at Venus. Now she wants to work here, at Babes."

"How's she look?"

Tony grinned his usual lecherous grin. "Sweet. *Real* sweet. I'm surprised the old man let 'er go."

"I'm sure he didn't wanna stand in her way." It wasn't like the old man to keep a girl if she wanted to make tracks. Especially since there were so many other great-looking babes running around out there. "She there?"

"Wanna talk to her?"

"Sure."

Tony handed the girl the cell.

"Hey, babe."

"Hello, Mr. Baroni." She certainly *was* sweet. She was also gorgeous, with light brown hair and beautiful deep blue eyes. Her smile made him uncomfortable, and he began squirming in his seat.

A good sign for a dancer, of course. It meant a shitload of revenue from repeat business.

But right now, it meant something else. Something he just wasn't in the mood for right now...

"What's your name?"

"Lisa, sir. Lisa Frohman."

Sexy, low-pitched voice. Another good sign. This babe could torment a guy in seconds. And if she'd come from Venus, she knew all the right moves. The old man always had great taste in babes and never hired dogs. Even so, Frank had to see her work.

"Got a video of your work?"

"Yes, sir. It's on YouTube. Just put in my name."

"One sec..." He flicked on his laptop, went into YouTube, and punched in her name. There she was, wearing nothing but gold stars and the tiniest pink G-string he'd ever seen. And she was moving like a pro.

Then the camera moved in on her face and settled there.

Frank stiffened. *Shit.* The same face, the same hair...

And those killer blue eyes...

But was it *her*? Was it really *her*?

How *could* it be? If it was, wouldn't she have betrayed herself just a few minutes ago, when she was looking at him? She should have at least blushed...or shown a little fear. *Some*thing should have shown in those eyes, right?

At twenty-two, even a seasoned hooker wouldn't be able to hide something *that* obvious...

He stopped the video and took a few breaths. Then he picked up the cell and tried extra hard not to glare when he looked at her this time. "You weren't, by any chance, at Schiller's Steakhouse on Colonial about six weeks ago, were ya?"

A shrug. "No, sir."

No betrayal in the eyes...

That's a *good* thing, right?

"You're sure about that? Six weeks is a long time. Maybe you forgot."

"I don't believe I've ever gone there. I really don't go to restaurants that serve seafood, Mr. Baroni. I'm allergic to shellfish."

Frank put the cell down. He sat back and rubbed his eyes.

"Boss? You still there?"

This can't be happening. It just can't be!

"Boss? You okay?"

Wake up. People will think you're having a damned stroke.

267

He picked up the cell. His heart was going to town once again. He took a breath and sighed heavily. "I'm fine, just fine."

"What do I tell this babe?"

"Giver her our schedule rundown and tell her she can start anytime."

"Catch ya later, Boss."

"Yeah."

Click.

Frank sat there, staring at the blank screen. Then it dawned on him.

YouTube. Of course!

Why the fuck hadn't he thought of it before?

He went back into it and found the videos. He spotted the one that showed the closeups he needed, so he brought it back to the accident scene, skipped the first few minutes until he found the shot with the cab, then settled on the babe standing next to the guy in the good suit.

"Turn around, baby…" His heart was racing. He desperately wanted a drink but told himself he could wait until he found out for sure. "Look at me, dammit. *Look* at me. I'm *here*! *Do* it to me!"

As if on cue, the figure in the video turned to face the camera.

Frank instantly froze the screen and zoomed in. And felt his heart sink heavily.

There she was again—that gorgeous face, those enormous blue eyes…

Frank closed his eyes and forced his memory to bring back the image of the babe who had walked out of his office just eight hours ago.

It took him only a moment to realize that the woman who had left his office was not the one in the video. The hair was different. The hair, the nose, the cheekbones, the lips. The eyes were similar, but this just wasn't the same woman.

And neither was the young dancer babe, Lisa Frohman.

The woman he was looking at right now seemed to resemble his wife as well as one of the pole dancers in the club. And when she turned away for a moment, then turned back to the camera, she resembled a girl Frank had known years ago, in high school. Her name was Alison, and they'd gone to a couple of the school's football games together. They'd been serious about one another until—

Damn it all to hell!

He clicked off, reached into his bottom drawer, and pulled out a fresh Scotch bottle. His pulse thundered loudly in his head as he broke the seal and poured a generous amount of the fiery liquid into his glass.

This was it. The Last straw. He just couldn't put up with this kind of shit much longer without completely losing his nut.

It was definite. He would definitely need to schedule another damned appointment with the doc, after all.

EPILOGUE

That evening, as Julie lay beside Robert in bed, she could easily feel the extreme happiness emanating from him.

Her memories of their meeting would forever remain crystal clear.

For some inexplicable reason, terrific things had resulted from that single bizarre encounter. The near perfect exchange of words and emotion. The pleasant camaraderie in the taxi ride. The strong sense of a wonderful bond that had developed almost immediately between them. Then, and most important, the strangely magical turn of events that had enabled them to escape certain death...

Since then, a love had grown between them that, to her, didn't seem possible. The moment she tried analyzing it, she realized that everything that had happened had been the result of her gift. And even though this special blessing had frightened her when she was a little girl, she fully understood that it was what had made her the person she had grown to become. It also made her realize that this gift had changed Robert as well, making him the man he had always wanted to be. Because of all that had happened, he discovered how wonderful life could be. And due to the strength of their ever-growing love, he honestly believed nothing bad could ever happen to them as long as they were together.

Was her grandmother their supernatural protector?

Or was all this merely that extra bit of sunshine the dear lady had told her about?

She had no idea. All she knew was that she had never been happier. She also knew that she wouldn't have changed anything that had taken place from the time she'd gotten off the plane to the moment she'd met Robert. She strongly believed that the extra bit of sunshine she had been holding in her hand all her life would always be there and never dim.

She also knew that the most wonderful guy she had ever known was lying beside her, thinking the same wonderful things.

"I totally agree," she said softly, smiling as she watched him.

"What was that?"

"I wouldn't change anything, either."

He gawked at her but said nothing . She wanted to smile because she could tell what he was thinking. He was afraid she had read his mind again. But instead of being frightened, as he would have been not long ago, he found it very amusing, even sexy.

"You read my mind again, didn't you?"

She shook her head. A thick curtain of brown hair spilled down the pillow, gathering in front of her face. "I told you I can't do that, didn't I?"

As always, she experienced that special thrill by letting him gently push the hair away. "You sure did."

"Then why do you sound so skeptical?"

"Because I believe you lied to me. And I am really and truly skeptical."

"After all I've told you—"

"Yes. After all that."

"And you still think I *can* read minds?"

"I only know you can read mine."

"Yours is special."

"You're humoring me…"

"But it's true."

"How special?"

"The most special mind I've ever known."

"Seriously?"

She nodded. "Seriously special."

"So quite naturally, you felt the need to read it."

She wrinkled her nose. "Just a teensy-weensy part of it. As I keep telling you, I see through emotion."

"Then these emotions of mine tell you all about what's going on inside this melon?"

"More or less…"

"And this is what tells you which parts you have to concentrate on once you decide to start poking around?"

"Yes. That, and a little intuition."

"You really expect me to believe that?"

"I'm hoping you will."

His eyes stayed on her, and she sensed his aura growing brighter. She could tell he was thinking that she was the only woman he ever wanted to share his life with. And that if she really wanted to mess around with his head once in a while, he didn't mind it at all.

"Julie?"

"Yes?"

"That was a crock."

She smiled sheepishly. "I was hoping you wouldn't notice."

"It was kind of obvious."

"Mad at me?"

"Not yet."

"What'll it take?"

"A lot more than that."

You deserve the best, child, her inner voice said, *and it looks like all things good and wonderful have begun happening.*

I miss you, she thought, holding back a tear. *I always will.*

We will be together once again, when it's time…

I hope so…

I have never lied to you, my child…

I know.

Now take that tiny bit of sunshine you've been given and use it…and use it well…and often…

I will. I promise.

"Robert?"

"Yes?"

"Get over here."

He blinked. "I'm already right here. Beside you. In the same bed. With you. And we're both naked—which, right now, is awfully convenient. And, from over here, extremely delicious."

"Yes, but you're not in the right spot."

"And where would *that* be?"

"I think I'd like you to find it yourself."

He moved closer and kissed her, long and passionately. "How's that?"

"Getting warmer."

"Warmer, hell. I'm sizzling right now."
"Then get closer and set me on fire, too."
"It'll be a pleasure..."

OTHER WORKS BY DAVID BERARDELLI

THE APPRENTICE
STEPPING OUT OF MY GRAVE
COLORS
IN ANOTHER REALM
BEYOND RECOGNITION
THE NIGHTMARE COLLECTOR
BEYOND GUILT
ENLIGHTENMENT
REDEMPTION
A RIPPLE IN TIME
YESTERDAY'S JOURNEY
AWAKENED
WINTER SCENE
THE PLANNING COMMITTEE
DEMON'D!

Titles available through:
Fiction4All